SEARCHING FOR BRIAN

BY WILLIAM SHORE

PAGE PUBLISHING, INC.
New York, NY

First originally published by Page Publishing, Inc. 2014

ISBN 978-1-63417-538-8 (pbk)
ISBN 978-1-63417-539-5 (digital)

Printed in the United States of America

1

I hadn't heard from my son, and it was four days past the end of spring break. He was a second-semester sophomore at a local university, and he had taken his classes seriously from the start.

I was worried and had no clues about where he might be. It was time for me to search for my son. A logical starting point was his dorm room. I called his roommate, Marty, and we arranged a meeting.

Coming through the door, I saw a disordered, cluttered apartment. It was hard for me to believe that only two people occupied it. The message here seemed to be a forfeiture of responsibility.

Marty was obviously anxious about dealing with me. He apologized for the surroundings but made no attempt to pick up.

He guided me to a coffee table that was beneath the only window. I sat in a rickety chair.

Marty started out. "Dr. Davis, I want to make something very clear. I don't know where Brian is."

"All right, Marty. But maybe you can recall something that could lead me to him. Something he said or did. I mean, maybe you know it without knowing it."

"I took a course in psychology. You're talking about the unconscious mind. Right?"

"You could say that, Marty." I cleared my throat and tried to recall my undergraduate years.

"I'm ready," he said.

"Were there any new friends in his life? A girlfriend?"

Marty hesitated. Then he spoke, "He brought a girl back here. Just a few times. Her name was Julie. But she stopped coming over, so I guess they broke up."

I said, "Did you notice any changes in his habits?"

"Yeah. He smoked a little more weed. No harder drugs, they didn't appeal to him. He did drink more, switching from beer to liquor, especially that Irish whiskey, Jamesons. I was with him at the bar on Route 1. He downed the shooters, more than I could believe. Then he passed out and fell to the floor. After I helped him up, he asked me to take him to his car. I wouldn't. With him driving, it would have been crazy. I took him back to our dorm. That was the only time he did that. I think."

Something must have been troubling Brian. He didn't seem preoccupied when we talked over the phone recently. But he was prone to keeping problems to himself.

I said, "Did you feel like your relationship with him had changed?"

"A little. He was out more with other guys. I don't know what he did with them."

Marty's long curly red hair fell down over his ears and forehead. He reminded me of a cocker spaniel. The inconspicuous kind that curls up on the couch. He said, "I'm kind of worried about him too. I'll do whatever I can."

I steered the conversation toward neutral topics in an attempt to relax Marty and obtain as much relevant information as I could. We talked baseball, the economy, his classes. Then I turned toward current events.

"This may be difficult, Marty, but I need to talk about Brian's drug use. I know he has been using the usual for college students: alcohol, mainly beer, and marijuana. That's why I must ask you, did you and Brian often do drugs together?"

"Not a lot. It was just a few times."

"Are you sure?"

"Hey, come on, this sounds like the Inquisition."

"Marty, please, I don't care about drugs you've taken. I want to get a better picture of Brian's behavior, especially what he was doing before he vanished."

"Well, I can tell you he was here less and less often."

I said, "Did you feel that Brian was distancing himself from you?"

"I guess so. It stung a little. Real friends are hard to come by around here."

The next thing was to inspect Brian's room. I examined cabinets and drawers.   There was no sign of drugs, no slips of paper with phone numbers or e-mail addresses.

The laptop yielded nothing. I was denied access because I lacked the password. Marty did not know it either.

I turned to Marty. "Where did he go for spring break?"

"It was Ocean City. He told me that." He nodded his head to convey certainty.

I said, "Where in Ocean City?"

"He didn't tell me, Dr. Davis."

2

I crossed the bay at 6 PM on Friday. It was spring, too early in the year for the crowds of vacationers. Driving was easy.

There was a sign indicating the police center was to the right, south, in the heart of the resort town. I knew about police work, how the brass left right about 5. First thing in the morning, I would be walking through their door.

Whenever I came to Ocean City, I remembered flying kites with Brian on the beach. When he was a child, Brian would run along with its flight, flapping his hands, exhorting it to stay up. Often, we walked about four miles, half the way to Bethany Beach, not knowing how far we'd come.

Today, people accompanied their frolicking dogs along the water's edge. Some of the animals waded into the water, wagging their soaked bodies, tails pointing upward, front legs churning like wagon wheels on a downslope.

This was a magical place enjoyed by sun worshippers, sailboat lovers, and surfers. There was an unspoken reverence for the ocean and its vagaries. Its visitors surrendered to a natural and unknown god.

The sun was starting to set, turning fiery red with a pink aura.

With my mind open and relaxed, I pondered options. I had no idea where Brian had stayed, and with hundreds of possible sites, the chances of finding the right one was remote.

He most likely had driven his old Celica down here. It was showing signs of advanced aging. But if he had taken it to a repair shop, which one?

The only place I could think to go was a diner, called Dempsey's, on the strip paralleling the ocean. I had taken Brian there. He liked it because they served him beer without an ID.

It wasn't far. There was a friendly ocean breeze, so I opened the top of my Audi. I could see the ocean sand to the left. On the right were beach wear stores, motels and miniature golf courses, with dinosaur and Hawaiian themes.

I found Dempsey's and, in a quiet booth, drank a couple while I read a bestseller apparently left behind by a customer. It was about a teen on the run from crooked lawyers.

When the waitress arrived, I asked her to circulate a photo of Brian to customers. She did, but no one recognized him. She walked behind the counter and showed the photo to employees. Again, there was no reaction.

Sarah, the waitress, had another idea. "Sir, you should stay maybe another hour, when the night manager comes in. His name is William."

I asked her what he looked like. "You can't miss him. He's fat, short, about like this." She put a flat hand out and raised it to her chin. "Very short. Thick glasses and 'roving hands.' He's pretty pathetic, sir, but you didn't hear that from me."

I nodded.

Later on, I spotted him at the cash register talking to a coiffed blond with an ample bosom. She didn't seem to mind having William's face rubbing up against her chest.

I paid my bill and introduced myself. William extended a puffy hand to shake. It felt like expanding dough. He said, "Edith told me about a guy looking for his lost son. Is that you?"

"That's right. Would you look at this photo and see if you remember him coming in for something to eat?" He turned it around to look at the back side, then viewed the front.

"You know, I have seen him before. He was with a kid who wasn't wearing shoes. A scruffy kid. They joked around like they knew things nobody else knew. Your son paid their bill. On the way out, whats-his-name?"

"Brian. Brian Davis."

"Brian dropped a pack of cigarettes. They were Marlboros. A red and white box, I'm sure it was. With plenty of smokes left. The other kid gave him a kitchen match to light up. You can't smoke in any restaurants in this state. I was about to tell them that, but as I approached, they left."

I checked into a hotel on the beach, the kind that rises to the clouds, beige and glass. The room was on the ocean side. There was a steady seaward breeze bending the willow branches toward the agitated waves.

I fell into bed, where my mind would not shut off. Using a hypnotic technique, I tried to free my mind. I pictured myself on my sailboat, way off the coast in calm waters. It wasn't working.

I watched a popular series, wishing I had a bottle of scotch. My cell rang. Looking to the table clock, it showed 4:32.

I picked up. It was Marty.

"Mr. Davis, I thought I should call you. Have you found him?"

"Not yet, Marty. Do you have something for me?"

"I was sorting through my e-mail and found one from Brian."

"Tell me what it says."

"He said he was heading up to Baltimore, and the message was dated April 28, the last day of spring break, Sunday, this week."

"What else?"

"He's going to be with a girl named Sherrie. He'll be back at school, in his classes, by Tuesday."

Today was Friday. He was three days late.

I was excited and wanted to check out of the room. But I needed some rest. I had to be able to concentrate through a long day in Baltimore.

Under the bedsheets, I finally surrendered to sleep.

Soon, a vivid nightmare riveted my mind.

I felt as if I had awakened in some kind of spinning glass chamber underground. I tried but could not speak. The spinning stopped, and I saw Brian running along a street above me. He kept turning his head to see who was behind him. There was a look of panic on his face.

Someone was chasing him.

I tried to get out of the chamber, but the sides were smooth and there was nothing to grip.

Suddenly, I was home, looking out the window to the front yard. Brian ran from his car and came to the door. He fumbled in his pocket for a door key. But the pocket was empty.

He banged on the door, but there was no sound. I was unable to move. A man in a black coat ran up behind Brian. He pulled out a long saber and plunged it through Brian's back. The end of the knife protruded out of his chest.

I was back in the chamber. It began to spin. I was buffeted about, and my body tumbled out of control. There was nothing I could do but scream, "Nooooooooooooooo!"

I awakened. My heart was beating like I'd run a sprint. Was the dream a premonition? I had a panicky feeling that I had to go to Baltimore, fast.

It was still dark out. It didn't matter. I ran around stuffing belongings into my bag and threw what I had in the Audi's trunk.

The road was mine. The engine emitted a sweet purr at seventy-five miles per hour.

The sun rose over a wooded lake near Sandy Point. I was hungry for breakfast but didn't know of a nearby restaurant that served it.

A convenience store loomed ahead. I bought minidonuts and coffee and consumed them outside my car.

3

It was a short trip to the Baltimore Beltway, which I reached by nine in the morning. Halfway around, there was a sign for a low-cost motel chain, with directions to its local offering.

The room was decent. After putting clothes and toiletries away, I plugged the cell into an outlet. Glancing at the phone, I noticed a message from my ex, Molly. The gist of it was that she wanted to speak to Brian but had tried him numerous times without getting through to him. "Call me, I have to know what's going on."

I spread out on the ample bed and fell asleep immediately, despite being serenaded by a trucker testing valves on his sixteen-wheeler.

The phone woke me. I said out loud, "Leave me alone." I let it ring four times and checked its window. It was Molly again. I picked up the phone and called her back.

"Dan, have you been able to talk to Brian?" She was never one for small talk.

"No, not yet."

"How long has it been since you heard from him?"

"Over eight days ago."

"Where are you?"

"I just drove from the shore to the outskirts of Baltimore. I checked into a motel."

"Why are you there? Brian hasn't been in Baltimore in years." I felt like I was a student being admonished by his primary school teacher.

I said, "One of Brian's roommates told me that he was coming up here."

She was frustrated with me. "Well how on earth do you expect to find him?"

"I'll meet with law enforcement soon. It's just a matter of time before they locate him. I'll call you if I find out anything more."

"No you won't. You won't call me. Either you forget or you procrastinate. I'm always the one who calls you."

From past experience, I knew the longer we talked, the more upset she would become. All I could do was wait for a break in the conversation. When it happened, I told her I had to leave and hung up.

She called me three more times, but I cut off the ringer.

It was close to nightfall. I wanted to make contact with the city police to set up a face to face. When I got through to a sergeant at headquarters, I was placed on extended hold. This was familiar to me, having consulted with law enforcement agencies in two counties.

I hung up and called again. No ring this time, just air. Feeling restless, I slid into the Audi and brought the engine to life. I reached across the dash and programmed the GPS.

It guided me through the complexities of a city filled with sudden turns and one-way streets.

I pulled into a serpentine underground lot filled with reserved parking and orange-striped saw horses. The Audi barely fit into a space for compact cars, made narrower by a Pontiac encroaching on my space. I sidled out of the car, careful not to inflict any scratches on the late model Chevy parked on the other side.

An imposing building loomed across the street. It had to be police headquarters. There was a tall set of metal doors, one cracked slightly ajar. As soon as I passed through, a woman in uniform glared in my direction.

"You got an ID, Mister?" She checked my license, handed it back to me, and asked the reason for my visit. I told her I was meeting a Detective Jackson. It was likely that at least one member of the force would have such a common surname.

She went to a computer screen and wrote something on a small piece of paper. It was a visitor's pass. After looking at directional signs, I walked up impressive marble steps.

I arrived at a second checkpoint, where my photo was taken and placed in laminate plastic, on a chain, around my neck. There was another staircase and a wide hallway, where clumps of men dressed in sport jackets and ties walked purposefully down the steps. At the landing, I noticed another set of signs on circular metal posts announcing Administration, Complaints, Waiting Area. I found no signs for the detective squad.

Further down the hall, I noticed a female officer talking on a phone. Finally, she hung up. She looked at me in disparaging fashion, her head tilted, eyes wide. "What is it?" I asked her where the detective unit was located. She didn't hear me. Her phone rang again. She said, "We don't do that here. Take him to the station on Lombard. He is in handcuffs, isn't he?" She suddenly ended the call. I tried again.

"Officer, can you tell me where the detective squad is located?"

"Do you have an appointment with a certain one?"

I thought, what if Detective Jackson wasn't in? "No."

"In that case, you have to wait on a bench over there. Take this." She gave me an orange card with a number at the bottom. "I'll call your number when it's time. Be prepared to wait a while."

The bench was long and filled with people. I chose the marble floor, with my back against a wall. To kill time, I fiddled with my handheld. Soon bored, I counted to three hundred by sevens. Sleepiness crept over me.

A woman's voice broke the quiet, shouting out my number. I was ushered to a door requiring a code before opening. An officer punched in the numbers while blocking my view.

Once through, a strong smell assaulted me. A cloud of smoke hovered over the room like the smog in Los Angeles. Ahead at a desk, two men were leaning back and puffing on Havana's best. Long ones, the kind that fall out of ash trays.

Navigating around the fog, I found a man in a sports jacket and dress pants. As he saw me coming, a look of curiosity shown on his face.

He stood up. The man looked to be in his forties. His black hair was combed back. He wore a genuine and welcoming smile.

"I'm Detective Sal Novelli." We shook hands. "You are?"

"Dan Davis."

"What do you do in the world, Mr. Davis?"

"I'm a psychologist in private practice, in Montgomery County."

He moved his arm. "Have a seat. So, what can I do for you?"

I explained.

He said, "Do you have a picture of him?"

I nodded.

"Let me see it."

I fumbled in my pocket and extracted my wallet. Brian's photo, slightly crumpled, was relatively intact.

He looked at it intensely, as if he were memorizing Brian's features. "Is he still wearing his hair long like this?"

"Yes."

"Age?"

"Twenty."

"Tell me the basic info, then we'll add some flavoring to it."

"Okay. I divorced his mother seven years ago. We had loud arguments, but nothing physical. It had to have affected him. He started staying overnight at his friends' houses."

"Does his mother live close by?"

"No. She moved to Ohio. I think she's there to stay. He's angry at her, so he refuses to go out to see her."

"Did either of you remarry?"

"She did. I don't know much about him. He's a businessman of some kind."

"And you, Doc?"

"I have a casual relationship. Nothing serious."

He said, "Back to Brian. Are there any other relatives he might have gone to spend time with?"

"No, we both come from small families, neither of which took any special interest in my son."

A phone rang. Sal hung up after a short exchange and retreated to a snack area to make an outgoing call.

I felt pleased about finding a cop who seemed competent. He asked good questions.

Sal returned with a wide smile. "My daughter just won an art award."

"Is she in high school or college?"

"She goes to a fancy prep school, on a scholarship. Anyway, let's get back to Brian."

"Look, Sal, I have to run this by you. I've been asking myself this question. What are the chances you'll find him, alive?"

"I'm sure it's over 60 percent. Often cops find them, after somebody calls in a tip."

"And the other 40 percent?"

"Maybe half aren't found, some because they left the city. The other half . . ."

Dan did the math. One in five was found dead.

Novelli said, "Look, Doc, you can't think like that. You have to be positive. Keep telling yourself he *will* be found alive. Okay?"

I had nothing to say. I was frightened.

"Let's stay focused. Answer me this. Does Brian have any health problems? Diabetes, other chronic illnesses?"

"None. He's in excellent health."

We continued on through Brian's friendships and dating history, including details of his relationship with Sherrie. I told him I was here because one of Brian's friends received a message that he was coming here to visit a previous girlfriend named Sherrie.

"Sherrie who, Dan?"

"I don't recall." It occurred to me that I had taken their picture when we had dinner together. It would be in my phone.

There it was. The two of them together. He studied it.

"What we do now, I want you to send it to Vice, at this number, from me. Here's my card. Tell them to ID Sherrie, no last name. I can just about guarantee you she's in their database." Sal looked spent. He said, "My hand needs a rest, Dan." He put the pen aside. "Let's break. What say I buy you a primo meatball sub at an original paisano restaurant, just a few blocks away? It's good exercise, and I can show you some of the Inner Harbor."

"That sounds good. But tell me, what did you mean when you said we'd add a little flavoring to the information gathering?"

"Sometimes, the most important stuff we learn about a missing person is his quirks, odd habits, that sort of thing. Or a big event in his life that you remember off the top of your head. Capisce?"

"I take it you're a pedigree Italian American."

He grinned. "A brilliant deduction, Doc."

There were many Brian stories. One quickly came to mind. "I'll tell you a revealing one, Sal. Brian started showing athletic talent when he was seven or eight. He would take a soccer ball and twirl it on a finger. And kick the ball with great accuracy into the net, with a friend playing goalie. I also recall how he jumped in a pool and taught himself how to swim. And swim well, with a natural motion."

"You serious? Does he still play soccer?"

"He's been diagnosed with ADHD. So, to answer your question, no, he doesn't. He's always been impulsive, jumping from one pursuit to another. I suspect this acting without planning has something to do with the fix he's involved in now."

"What do you mean by the fix he's in?"

"I've run so many scenarios through my head. But it's all speculation. I need to stop doing that."

"What about drugs?"

"He's used what the typical middle class teen has. I'm almost certain he hasn't used street drugs to any excess. But alcohol, well, I've seen him come home from parties obviously intoxicated. Then, for awhile, there's a decrease in consumption." I probed for other memories. One came back. "I found marijuana accessories, a bong and a roach clip, in his room in plain sight. We've been lenient parents, so he knew there'd be minimal punishment at best, or none at all. Looking back, I'm sure we should have placed some restrictions on his drug use. There should have been some consequences for smoking in the house."

Sal said, "Even with leniency, he didn't graduate up to the stronger drugs."

"That's true," I said. "But there was a trespassing charge, and shoplifting at two record stores. He likes taking risks, for the thrill of it. When he was twelve, he climbed a long ladder at an industrial plant, all the way to the roof, on a dare. A grounds man chased him, but he got away."

15

"Any serious injuries in childhood, or teen years? A broken arm, leg?"

"None."

Sal stubbed out his cigarette. He said, "Now tell me one of your favorite Brian stories."

I cleared my throat and took a sip of water. "In middle school, he ran during a PE class, and they clocked him. His time was faster than anybody's in the school. So the coaches wanted him on the track team when he moved up to high school."

"How did you feel about that?"

"I don't know. Bafflement, probably. I considered all of our relatives, on both sides, and there wasn't a single athlete. All I do is sail, for fun. Competition never appealed to me."

Sal said, "I think with natural athletes, they have a mind brimming with confidence. They get a thrill out of proving they're number one. Did you see that tendency in Brian?"

I said, "Not really. He's a free spirit. It goes along with the impulsivity."

"That makes sense, Dan. He's definitely an interesting kid."

I continued with the story. "He learns about how to run, the strategies and conditioning. In tenth grade, he runs varsity and nearly every one-hundred and four-hundred-meter race. A coach told me he was potentially Olympic class."

"Did you think that?"

"I did, when Brian was running. But otherwise, it would never happen. I knew his pattern. He started missing practices. The more they disciplined him, the more he resisted. I met with his coaches and faculty members, and they told me about it, wanting my help. But nothing, restrictions or incentives, did any good."

"So they took him off the team?"

I nodded. "He rebelled as a way to show them he would defy their 'dumb rules,' as he called them. He cooked up a plan with a friend on the cross country team, a practical joke of sorts."

"Practical joke?"

"It's hard to believe," I said. "The other boy, Eddy, gave Brian an outfit for the race. He puts it on, sneaks behind everybody into thick woods and shrubs."

"Did you see this?"

"No, Sal, I was working. Anyway, about halfway through the race, he joined the runners, in last place. In a couple of minutes, they came out into a meadow. Brian ran fast and went to the head of the pack."

"You got a ballsy kid, Doc. Like my fifteen-year-old."

"The best runner in the county is about 40 feet behind Brian. The boy accelerates, goes all out to catch up, but can't do it. He loses his wind and drops back. Because Brian is far ahead, the other boys maintain ground but don't sprint forward.

Now it's Eddy's turn. He runs fast, beyond the others, until he is maybe 30 feet behind Brian. Close to the finish line, Brian slows and lets Eddy go ahead and split the ribbon."

Sal said, "Then they had all this figured out. Brian fixed the race so his buddy would win."

I nodded.

"Wow! I gotta hand it to your son, Dan. That was a clever strategy."

I was incensed. "You approve of my son's cheating? Brian was caught and suspended, and no athletics for one season. What he did was wrong. It's all part of an engrained pattern. He excels at something, then loses interest, is disciplined, and undermines his progress."

"From where I sit, it also means he's a thrill-seeker. That's what's most important for me to know."

"So you think that knowing about this kind of behavior could help you with the investigation?"

"It sure can. Now, let's move on to college. Are his grades okay? B or C average?"

"That's about right. He's passed every course."

Sal looked away, abstracted. "What we have here is a very smart and clever guy who enjoys trying to outwit others. Not out of spite, out of sport. For the fun of it."

I mulled that over and said, "I hadn't thought of it that way. But now that I do, your argument is plausible."

Lunch consumed, we went our separate directions. Sal went back to the police building. I found a bookstore, but when I walked in, I realized I was not in the mood to read. I looked out the window, hoping to spot my son.

4

The next day was Wednesday. Clear and windy. The weather lady on local TV forecast a chance of rain. In a cynical mood, I wondered if she was playing it safe. What she said was like thinking that a client of mine *may* lapse into psychosis. It meant nothing, really.

We met up at the Inner Harbor, in front of a bookstore trumpeting a storewide sale. To advertise such a sale was deceptive. But also good psychology. If all books were discounted, the store would lose too much money. "Storewide" was the false claim. If I were to look around, I would find some books costing full price. "Sale" was often just a ruse to pull customers into the store.

"Hey, buddy, are you ready to rock and roll?" Sal approached with a beaming smile, as if he had just seen a long-lost relative. "I'm betting this Sherrie person lives on the East side. It's pretty cheap to live there, and some areas are crawling with users."

The unmarked Chevy sedan was obviously government issue, dark blue. One that blends into the road like a lizard in the woods.

Sal was a cautious driver, courteous to pedestrians, to the point where cars behind him beeped their displeasure.

We had to go through a few center-city communities. Novelli said, "For the next couple miles, we'll be in scenic Inner Harbor. Are you familiar with it?"

I said, "It's the attraction that led to the renaissance of Baltimore."

"In a sense, that's true. There it is on your right. Mayor Schaefer, he was one cantankerous SOB. You didn't cross him. He pretty much pushed the project through despite friction between developers, banks, contractors, and unions. It got done mainly because nobody wanted to be blamed for sinking the ship."

I said, "I saw the statue of Schaefer over there."

"Right, where he's walking fast like he has a big meeting, dressed in a trench coat. Beaming like a wolf in the henhouse."

Sal parked in a prohibited zone with a clear view of a World War I freighter docked at the Harbor. Novelli said, "Most think the Inner Harbor was responsible for bringing the city back. It wasn't. The best thing about the harbor was it actually created lots of cooperation. Communities stopped fighting each other, and for awhile, politicians buried their swords. They worked with Schaefer to improve this whole city, even if they hated him. Street crime went down, city streets got fixed, schools improved. You should have been here." We slowed at a red light.

"Anyway, Doc, the prosperity lasted maybe a decade. Since then, the city's gone through a period of neglect and rampant corruption. The crime rate is way up. Gangs control over 10 percent of Baltimore. Drug-related violence keeps homicide rates through the roof. Kids twelve years old are being recruited to move drugs and run errands for gang members. It's ugly, with no end in sight."

I said, "So the police department is being stretched to the max."

"It has been. But recently, that's improved a little," he said.

We moved slowly eastward, leaving downtown and approaching ethnic neighborhoods. A large park loomed ahead, with an obelisk near the middle. Sal said, "That's a war memorial from World War II." Sal turned onto a cobblestone street, and I could make out a second park on a slope. It leveled out to display two soccer fields. "This is an enclave of Russian Americans. Working class, mainly. They protect the neighborhood from outsiders. They're prejudiced as hell against blacks. Very conservative. The worst ones are skinheads." He pointed. "There's one, at the bus stop. See the tattoos up and down the arms?"

The man wore a long beard, T-shirt, thick fitting jeans, and storm-trooper boots. Sal said, "Do you think he's a good candidate for deep analysis?"

I smiled at him. He said, "Now we're entering East Baltimore. It's an interesting ethnically mixed place." I looked to the opposite side of the street, where there were stores with names like Arturo's Bodega, Soul Kitchen, Polack Jonny's.

"Keep in mind, the street we're on, Patterson, is a kind of dividing line between the middle class and the poor." He pointed to the left. "On that side is the African American community. It's in a lot better shape than it was twenty years ago because regular people like me and you bought up houses, got them renovated, then sold them back to new homeowners with decent to average credit ratings. But drugs remain a curse. From young ages, these kids watch what's happening around them. They see guys getting out of expensive cars, wearing expensive clothes, flashing rolls of twenties. These kids, they're like soldiers, they do whatever they have to do to impress the bosses. Most youngsters die or are sent to prison before they're twenty-one. Unbelievable, isn't it?"

"I think the problems that plague Washington are just as bad, Sal."

"And they don't like outsiders here, especially after dark. Cops have been shot at if they make the mistake of being alone."

He turned onto a cross street. "On the right side, there is sameness and order. Brooms by the steps where some sidewalks are swept every day. These people, Eastern Europeans, take pride in their houses and property. See how they diagonal park? Cars never encroach on their neighbor's space." Sal's phone beeped. "Give me a minute." He turned into a driveway and lifted the phone out of his pocket.

"Bingo. They have Sherrie's information. Listen up, Dan. It says she is Sherrie McClintock, age 28. Four drug arrests, a public intox. Total forty-eight days jail time."

I asked, "Is there an address?"

"Yeah, it's about three miles from here, just off Decker Avenue. But don't get your hopes up. These people move around."

Novelli drove due south on a wide boulevard, which he exited, then turned onto a narrow street with flat-roofed houses. He pointed. "A few houses up the block. "Here's the McClintock girl's place, over there, that unattached blue cottage. We'll park right here so if she's looking out the window, she won't see us pull up."

We walked slowly. When we reached the front door, there were quick footsteps of a man coming toward us from behind. Novelli pivoted. "You, right there, I'm a cop. Don't move another step forward." He drew his gun out of its shoulder holster.

The man slowed down. "Look, I'm just here to find my daughter, Sherrie McClintock. And I don't want anybody breakin' into her house."

"We're looking for your daughter, too." Novelli's voice was commanding.

Despite this, the man would not back down. "Now I know the law. Show me your warrant. If you don't have one, then get off my property."

Novelli said, "We don't need a warrant because there's probable cause. And there is no way we're going anywhere. If you don't like that, take it up with the district attorney."

He shot a glance at me. "Who are you?"

"My name is Dan. Your daughter Sherrie might be with my son, Brian. Brian Davis. He's been missing well over a week."

His voice conveyed scorn. "Look, I don't care about that."

Novelli had lost his composure. He said to McClintock, "I'm going in. Don't try to stop me, or you'll end up in the back of my car in handcuffs."

McClintock asserted, "Nobody's home. I been parked here all day. Her car isn't here. I knocked and knocked, and nobody came to the door."

I spoke to Novelli. "Why don't you stay out here? I'll go in with him."

Novelli shook his head. "That is a bad idea. What if somebody, a drug addict, is in there, with a handgun?"

I ignored the remark and faced McClintock. "Let's go inside. We can search the place and find out where both of them are."

His hands were on his hips, a frustrated expression on his face.

I said, "Can you find your way around the lock?"

McClintock stood still, eyes fixed, as if paralyzed with indecision. Then he reached into a pocket and extracted a key chain. He selected one, approached the door, and inserted it into the hole.

We walked in. Ahead was a narrow hallway, with clothing racks. Sprouting from one was a brown winter coat. Underneath it, on the floor, rested a pair of high-heeled boots.

McClintock said, "Sherrie, are you here?" He searched the living room and kitchen. I heard him say, "Like I told you, she's not here."

I went into the bathroom and bedroom. "She's not here either." My heart sank.

McClintock said, "I'm going to check the backyard." Out the window I could see him fight through tall grass. There were car parts on dirt patches. On a concrete porch, two metal chairs had rusted to green.

I heard Novelli coming through the front door, speaking into his phone. When he saw me, he asked if I had found anything. I shook my head. "I gotta go, Dan. It's a call that won't wait."

I said, "All right. I'll call a cab to the motel."

He nodded, turned quickly, and walked to his car.

I went back inside. There were footsteps in the kitchen. McClintock walked out and faced me. "A man can't even wait to see his daughter without losing his rights." He bellowed, "Get out!"

I said, "The detective left. It's only you and me." I tried to calm him by talking in collective terms. "We both have missing children. Maybe I can find out where the two of them went. I strongly believe they're together, a matched pair."

He seemed to be turning inside himself, a part trying to get out, to escape his private hell.

I proposed, "Ten minutes and I'll be gone."

He loosened. "Ten minutes is all you get."

The front door creaked open. It was Novelli. He whispered, "There'll be a squad car here in about half an hour. Listen to me. You can look, but *do not* touch or move anything. Wait for Detective Nance and a uniform to get here. They'll have a probable cause document. Focus on McClintock, get whatever useful information you can out of him. All right?"

I walked to the bedroom and opened the curtains. There was nothing but a steep sloping yard to the neighbor's property.

The bed was against a piece of drywall that was cracked and raw. I moved toward it. Sheets were askew. A pillow was half covered.

Often, users stashed drugs and paraphernalia in compartments or drawers near where they slept. So that when they woke up, the next high was at their fingertips.

Beside the bed was a square table, with one drawer in its place. Inside it were three containers of prescription medication, all labeled Dilaudid, a synthetic morphine-class drug. Its street name was Dils, one of the more popular antipain agents. There were no pills in any of the bottles.

What was most interesting was that all three of the labels were in Sherrie's name, but two different doctors had prescribed them at about the same time. She was either taking too many or selling some. I committed the information to memory and replaced them.

Besides some sweets in cellophane bags and two containers of spring water, the only thing of interest was a cell phone charger cable, missing the phone.

The bathroom looked curiously well kept. Towels were on racks, toilet and tiles scrubbed. In the medicine cabinet, there were the typical bottle of Tylenol and an antacid. Someone, probably a relative, was cleaning up to make the room serviceable for resident and family members.

I entered the living room. On a low table was the TV. Upon close inspection, there was a crack in the screen. A cheap futon was diagonal and facing away from the TV, and two throw rugs were lumped together. There was nothing but a stained carpet underneath. It smelled of cat urine.

I wandered in McClintock's direction. He was in the kitchen turning skillets and pans upside down. I stood facing him. He looked up and squinted at me without expression. "There's nothing but the usual in here. I checked every drawer. There's no microwave, and next to nothing in the refrigerator."

I tried for a sympathetic connection. "This must be terrible for you, searching your daughter's home. It would be intrusive to me if people were looking around in Brian's place."

He was pensive, staring intensely at the floor, as if his answers were written there.

I wanted to probe. Would he tell me anything about her childhood? I asked.

He replied, "She was a nice kid. Friendly with the other girls when she wanted to be. Then other times reserved. She had no close friends, so I thought she was lonely."

I said, "What kinds of things did she enjoy doing?"

"Her mom entered her in contests. She spent hours combing Sherrie's hair. It was shiny, like it had been lacquered."

"She and your wife were close?"

"Too close. When Nita was dying of cancer, both girls saw it. Sherrie took it harder. She stayed in her room, wouldn't go to school. She was fourteen when Nita died."

"Do you think she got over it?"

"She started to. Having boys ask her out helped. But the car wreck spoiled everything."

"Tell me about it."

He paused, considering whether to open this door. "A girl was driving and not paying much attention to the road. Sherrie was in the passenger seat. The car turned into traffic, and a pickup rammed into the car. Sherrie nearly died."

"Where were her injuries?"

"To her spine, mainly lower back. Nerves, muscle damage. That was when all her pain started. She went to more than one pain doctor, but nothing they did controlled it much. It wasn't fair, a nineteen-year-old girl having to go through that." He moved to an upholstered chair and rocked soothingly back and forth.

"She started making up stories. One was she got a part in a play in that theater at Fells Point. She never did. Then she convinced me to let her move into this place. I own it, but she took it over. And she wanted her privacy, hinting I should move to another place."

"So she could be pushy," I said.

"I'd come to visit, and she'd yell at me to go away. I wasn't welcome in my own house." He took out a crumpled handkerchief and blew his nose. Tears welled up, and he swept them away with a downward swipe.

There was nothing to say. A deep sadness engulfed me. Silence filled the room, adding anxiety to the sadness. I said, "I should have asked by now. What's your first name?"

"Mort. No middle name."

I said, "Mort, I met Sherrie once. When she was dating my son. He's in college at a Maryland University. Last year, when Sherrie and Brian were dating, the three of us went out to dinner. I liked her. They laughed a lot together."

Mort put the handkerchief in his pocket. His eyes were red.

I said, "I'm nearly certain they were together when they disappeared last week." I paused to let that sink in. Then, "Has Sherrie ever been missing this long?"

"She was gone over a month in rehab. No one even told me where she was. They cut ties, don't speak to me anymore. The whole lot of them."

"Is there anyone who might know where she is?"

"Sherrie lives on and off with her sister Claire. Her older sister."

I felt like I was running out of time. "Why not call her? She could have been in contact with Sherrie."

"I don't own a cell phone."

I took mine out, and attempted to hand it to him.

"Don't you know you can get radiation poisoning from those things?"

"Mort, I need to talk to Claire. What's her number?"

He balled up his fists and glared at me. "No. You talk to me, but I don't know you. Forget it."

"We have to do something. Do you have any other ideas?"

He bristled. "I have an idea to kick you out of here. You're making me lose my patience."

"Mort, maybe you know this. Let me tell you anyway. Sherrie has a drug abuse problem."

"Well, I don't see any clear evidence of it."

"There were three empty prescription bottles in her bedroom. I think she was doubling up on a powerful pain drug call Dilaudid."

"But are you sure? She could have been giving them to a friend who was in pain." His defenses were brittle.

I went to my wallet. "Here, look at Brian's photo."

The man held it loosely in the palm of his hand. "Never saw him before."

"Mort, every minute that goes by, my chances of finding him go down. Maybe we could join forces, so to speak, look for them together."

"I know my daughter. She's okay. She can take care of herself. Last year, she disappeared for two weeks. Then one day, I knocked on her door, and she was so pretty and couldn't have been any nicer to me."

His thoughts showed a deep distrust and a nearly complete unwillingness to act. These were hallmarks of a paranoid personality disorder.

I racked my brains for a strategy and found one. "Mort, if you're not worried about her, then why did you sit out in your car all day and night watching this place?"

"Only during the day."

"Can you drive me over to Claire's place? I'd like to talk to her."

"Aren't you supposed to be with the cops?"

"Look, if we leave now, that detective won't be here until we're gone."

Mort looked less defeated. He established eye contact, and his fingers balled into a fist. "Let's go."

Mort's old car door was rusted, and the door put up a fight when I tried to open it. When it finally gave, there were cans of oil, candy wrappers, paper cups, and a box of tools on the seat and the floor. He left it to me to transfer the junk to the back. His indolent behavior irritated me, but he was the only ride in sight. I would steel myself to reach the destination.

He slowly wheeled out into traffic. I said a few things, but he ignored me. Shifting about in his seat and clearing his throat, Mort seemed uncomfortable with a passenger in the car.

To deflect my mind, I visualized receiving the decisive tip that would lead to Brian's discovery. Even with such thoughts, I felt strangled by the total breakdown of contact with my son.

If Brian were holed up somewhere, with a girlfriend, he would have called me. That suggested he was being held against his will. But why? That was the dead end. He wasn't the type of person who would do something to another person that would spark retribution.

I could assume that Brian was without a cell phone. Or if he had one, it had run out of power. If somebody else had his cell, they would need the password. The phone company wouldn't tell the thief what it was. But captors could beat it out of Brian.

5

We pulled up at a small wood frame cottage with fading white paint. There was a bay window, more horizontal than vertical, partially obscured by a shrub. The front yard grass had not gotten off to a good start in the growing season. It was brown, and weeds were fighting for territory. There was a field on the right, and an awkward low masonry brick wall on the left, between properties.

Coming up behind me, Mort said, "Go in alone. I'm staying away." I sensed the years of mutual resentment that had built up after he walked out on his family.

I said, "You'll wait for me? Until I come back out of the house?"

"Of course. My car will be over there." He pointed halfway down the street.

I hit the front-door bell button. There were voices, but no one opened the door. Overcoming anxiety, I knocked. The door moved inward.

A slight redheaded woman opened the door a few inches. "Is that you, Donna? You know you can just come on in."

"Uh, my name is Dr. Davis, ma'am. Can I come in?"

She dropped what sounded like a laundry basket. A muffled slapping noise.

A hand wrapped itself around the door, and it opened. "What is a doctor doing at my house? I thought you people stopped making house calls."

"I'm not actually a medical doctor. I'm a psychologist. Are you Claire?"

She nodded. I told her why I was there.

"Since you're looking for my sister as well as your son, you can come in."

She led me into an area beside the kitchen, to a plastic table with four minichairs. A kitchenette. From the ceiling there was a bird cage suspended, with the door ajar. I eyed it with curiosity.

"Oh, that thing. My husband tried to clean it without opening the door. It fell, hit the floor, and the cage door opened, and out flew the canary. It's probably lying dead somewhere. Sit down."

She was a short overweight woman with wiry red hair. We sat. With a look of confusion, she asked, "How did you know where I live?"

"Your dad and I met when I went to look for Sherrie at her house."

I filled her in on the information I had gained about Sherrie's disappearance. She said, "You know, I haven't seen her for a while. You're getting me worried." She had a nervous habit of wringing her hands. After the wringing, she placed her arms around her torso in a comforting gesture.

A phone rang in another room. Claire rose up. "Excuse me. While I get that, Dr. Dailey, go into the living room. It's over there. It's more comfortable than here."

The entrance to the room was bordered by lines of beads extended from the top door frame. They emitted a swishing sound as I went through.

It was a square-shaped room with a long couch and adjacent wing chair. I could hear Claire. She was talking in an animated tone. It sent a surge of hopefulness through me. If Sherrie was calling, I could find Brian and have him home tonight.

She spent a while on the phone. I had to walk around, expending nervous energy. Through the bay window I could see a carport, where an old Chevrolet sedan was parked. One of the tires was being tended to by a man in white T-shirt and jeans and long brown hair.

I heard a baby crying and a door open.

In a few minutes, Claire walked into the room cradling her child. I was looking out the window.

To my back, she said, "Oh, that's Webb out there. He and my husband, Billy, are best friends."

"I see. Listen, Claire, was that Sherrie calling you?"

"Oh, no. It was the plumber. We have a leaky hot-water heater, and he's taking his time coming over here."

I could not hide my disappointment.

"Doctor, before I picked up, I hoped it was her too."

"If you don't mind, Claire, would you tell me her phone number so I can call it? We could get lucky."

"I don't think so. She lost another phone months ago. All you'll get is a 'This number is not in service' message."

"Well, can you give me her number anyway?"

I punched it into my phone's memory and made a note to call later.

Claire said, "She's done that before, come crying to me about losing her phone, asks me if she can borrow mine. Putting something of value in her hands is like kissing it good-bye."

We sat. "Doctor, tell me the truth. Do you think something bad has happened to them?"

"I don't know. I can't stop asking myself that."

Claire's eyes brightened. "Come to think of it, I remember she talked about a Brian. She didn't bring him over here. Where did they meet?"

I reflected. "That's a good question. I think he mentioned at a party in a little town, Olney, near where I live. Then I met Sherrie when the three of us had a meal at a restaurant in Baltimore."

"Where do you think they've gone, Dr. Davis?"

"I wish I could say. There's a city police detective named Novelli who's working with me. I think I gave him enough information to answer that for us, soon. Their crime information computer can be a big help, along with support staff like fingerprinting techs. I'm confident the case is moving forward."

"When it's city police, it's more likely to be moving sideways."

This concerned me. "You don't trust them?"

"It's more like, you can't rely on them. They work hard on something, then when they get stuck, they drop you like a hot potato. That's what happened when Billy got beat up bad at a bar."

As if to distract her mind from what she had brought up, she fumbled with an earring, detached it, and reattached it. She said, "This thing. No more earrings for me."

"But about your sister, what sorts of issues has she been dealing with lately?"

"Did my father tell you about her accident? And then getting addicted to pain medicine?"

"Only about the accident. You saw warning signs to the addiction?"

"She acted drowsy. I thought she was drunk at first. But then I would come over to her house. She has a sweet tooth, and I'd bring her pies or candy bars. After a while, there were these sleazy guys lying around. They weren't friendly, and sometimes they'd be asleep. On the couch or the floor. Now that I think of it, they were probably stoned."

"These seedy guys, do you know any names, or where they live?"

"No. She kept that all a secret. Like they weren't even there. I overheard her on my phone once. She was acting desperate, saying how bad she hurt, trying to talk one of them into getting her more pain medicine. She called it 'my stuff.' I knew what she meant. It was manipulation, pure and simple."

"So she's good at getting people to do what she wants."

"She always has been. Boy, has she made me do things I never should have done for her. She's so lazy. I doubt she's worked a real job for over two years. It's pathetic how she's got her father strung around her thumb. Do you know he doesn't make her pay any rent?"

Claire seemed envious of a sister who was under the grip of addiction. It was as if Claire were oblivious to the ways her life was so much better than her sister's.

She slapped her thigh. "Those gnats. They're a curse."

I said, "An exterminator could get rid of them."

Claire smiled. "I know. We have to hit the lottery first."

I said, "So, can we go back to Sherrie?"

"Yes, Doctor. Sometimes she needs to get away from her life, so she comes here, sleeping a lot, drinking beer. It's not good for her to be around my son. She suddenly loses composure, yells, talks out of her head. Billy had to tell her to leave a few times. He's got to where he can't stand her."

Sherrie caused tension, and probably conflict, between her sister and brother-in-law.

Claire said, "Don't get me wrong. I ache for my little sister, I love her and always will. But nothing seems to help. Doctor, do you treat patients like Sherrie?"

"I do, Claire. There are recognizable patterns of behavior, but every user is unique." I steered away from the generalities of clinical experience. "Let me ask you this. Where do you think Sherrie gets drugs?"

"She's so secretive. I'm sure she decided the less I knew, the less conflict there'd be between us. Me, I hate drugs. They've destroyed the lives of loved ones, friends."

"Do you think your husband can shed any more light on this?"

"Billy's fighting his own demons. Whatever you do, don't talk to him about this. It could set him off." She rubbed an earring, then tugged at it. "A man at the VA, he said it's PTSD. He got it when he was fighting in Iraq. Something damaged his mind."

"That can be very hard on the whole family."

She nodded. "I have to walk around on pins and needles. He gets very depressed, stays away from people. And sometimes, you can see the fear and anger in his eyes. He's holding whatever it is inside, and it's eating away at him. He's afraid to drive, thinks he's going to run somebody over and kill them."

"Then you must be afraid to be a passenger in the car with him."

The baby stirred. Claire had mothering to do.

I said, "I'm curious, Claire. What would you do if you were me? What would you choose to do to find your sister?"

"I'd drive by her place a few times a day and knock on her door. Knock long and loud, hoping and praying she's inside.

6

I was swimming in a pool of new information. Talking to Claire gave me several avenues to consider. I had to prioritize. Something I advised my clients to do but rarely did for myself.

I stared at a legal pad for an hour in the library. Nothing registered.

Hunger got the better of me. I had noticed an array of ethnic restaurants along a quiet street off Pratt, in Center City. Tired of driving, I hailed a cab.

I sampled food from three different countries. At a Jamaican restaurant, the waiter said, "Sir, would you like a bottle of our famous ginger beer?" I had three. They were cold, aromatic, and highly satisfying.

A sugar craving led me to a bowl of strawberry ice cream, bought out of the back of a catering truck business called Heavenly Creations.

It was a breezy evening suitable for walking. At the harbor, I encountered a national bookstore chain with two massive floors. The mysteries were on the second floor, but so was the heat. I left the store and found a bench near a teeming Pratt Street.

From my perch, I watched young couples amble lazily down a promenade.

My head cleared, and I decided to walk to the garage in which my car was parked. I was going to drive back to Sherrie's house.

With Mort out of the picture tonight, I would provide sole surveillance. If necessary, I was prepared to stay the whole night, watching from my car. No doubt Sherrie kept odd hours and could have, for the most part, become a nocturnal creature. It would benefit her. There were less people and more dark places to make drug transactions.

On the next block, I parked in front of an undeveloped lot with a cyclone fence. In the yard were unconnected planks, looking like a pier blown apart by a storm's battering waves.

Exiting my car, I hiked the short walk to Sherrie's front door, where I tapped and waited anxiously. There was no reaction. Then I applied several knocks, louder than the first ones.

I said in a raised voice, "Sherrie. Open the door. I'm not going away."

Silence.

Then, "Get out of here! Whoever the fuck you are. Now! My brother lives across the street, and he'll put a bullet through your head."

"My name is Dan, Sherrie. I just want to find my son, Brian. I know you. The three of us went out to dinner."

She waited. Slowly, the window curtains parted, then shut. I could hear her moving into the next room. Returning to the door, she pushed back the curtain again, saying, "Move your head down to the window." She flicked on a lighter. I could see her eye next to the flame.

The deadbolt clicked open, and I stood in front of her. "We go in there," she said, pointing to a darkened living room. When we reached it, she remained standing, staring fixedly into my eyes.

Her voice was angry and sullen. "Look, I don't know who you are. You could be the Wizard of Oz. And I don't know where Brian is. We were together a couple days, then he left. He had to go back to school. That's all I have to say."

Her movements were hurried, like those of a person who had taken a stimulant, such as methamphetamine, or cocaine. Under the influence of either one, she would behave like a fast-moving train without brakes.

"Sherrie, I went to the college. He is not there. This makes him over a week late. I just need to talk to you."

"Look, Mister, I have things to do, places to go, people to see. And they don't like to wait. Am I making myself clear? You don't have to answer if this is all over your head." She moved her flat hand front to back above her head. Raising her voice, she said, "We are growing tired of your babble." I glanced about the room, wondering who her accomplice was. There was nobody.

I needed leverage. Addicts were always looking for money. They had to, because of the cost of their habit. Adding to the problem was the fact that they often lost cash, putting it in places they could not remember. Or other users stole it. "Sherrie, I'm going out to get some money at an ATM. We'll split it. I know you have a pain condition. With the money, you can see a doctor and get some more medication."

"I need at least $400. For some bills to pay tomorrow."

I said, "Either give me a door key, or leave the door unlocked."

"Are you crazy? I won't give my door key to a stranger. I'm not going anywhere. Now get on the road."

It was a moonless night, with very few people on the streets. I drove toward street lights, and took a left onto a wide boulevard. A few blocks down, there was a bank sign. I withdrew the cash, and doubled back fast, fearing that Sherrie might impulsively embark on a drug-seeking journey. Addicts lied and had terrible judgment.

When I entered her house, she was singing a rock song face up on the bed, in an off-key voice. She stopped as I came into the hallway.

"What do you want? I told you to leave me alone." She had forgotten our talk. Memory loss was common among addicts who took too many stimulant drugs.

I said as gently as possible, "I've got your money, $200, for now." I held it in my hand. "I'll give you the other half later."

She came up from the bed cat quick and snatched the roll of twenties. In the same motion, she placed it under a pillow.

Raising her upper body, she assumed a sitting position, legs off the bed, bare feet on the floor. She was wearing nothing but sheer bra and panties. Looking at me with sultry chestnut eyes, she blew a kiss. I was transfixed. She was destructively beautiful.

The dance continued. She stood up and turned around, showing me a supple ass. Slowly taking off her panties, she said, "I know you like what you see. Why not take your clothes off and join me?"

My impulse was to throw her down on the bed and forcefully enter her.

I couldn't. "I won't do this. It is just . . . wrong."

She turned venomous. "So you're a proper gentleman who only screws his wife. If you have one. Don't guys like you get horny? You look like you want to screw my brains out. Or do you prefer guys?"

"Sherrie, you're going to get dressed and get in my car. Then you're going to help me find my son."

"I'm staying right here, Mr. Dan. To rest up. I was beaten and raped, and I can't remember anything."

If she'd lost her memory, how could she know she was beaten and raped? This was about getting even at me for spurning her offer.

Anger was tightening my chest. "If you don't do this, I'll take back every dollar I gave you."

"Then come and get it, asshole." She placed herself in a fetal position around the pillow. I fell upon her, then pushed her away. She sank to the floor. "You broke my back! You bastard."

I took the cash and stuffed it into a pants pocket. "You'll get the money back and more when you've done what I asked. All you have to do is drive around with me and look for anything, a street or a building, that looks familiar. You won't have to get out of the car. Let's go. Now!" She rocked back and forth. I went into the living room to calm down.

She was a highly manipulative and demanding child. If I waited too long, she would think of another ploy to frustrate me.

I faced her and said, "I'll give you ten minutes to get ready. If you waste time, I'll take that to mean you refuse to cooperate. Then all bets are off."

She said, "What's that supposed to mean?"

"It means I'll call a detective friend, and he'll take you to the big cop station and ask you one hundred questions while you go into withdrawal. By the way, what is your drug of choice? Meth or coke? With a painkiller?"

She lost her edge and put on street clothes over the underwear. Inside the Audi, she shut down. I looked at my watch. It was past eleven. The moon had retreated behind clouds, providing muted light. The street was faintly recognizable. Too much was under veil of darkness.

This was a stupid mistake. I had allowed anger to affect my judgment. "Look, Sherrie, we'll drive around in the morning. Tonight you sleep. If you don't have any more drugs, I'll do what I can to help you through withdrawal."

"Don't worry. I'll get by. And mind your own damn business."

7

"I'm looking, I'm looking." She had eaten little breakfast. Her demeanor was "just get this over with."

We were on Lombard Street in Southwest Baltimore. She told me this was a good place to start. I had asked, "Why here?"

"To go shop for clothing. What do you *think* I was doing?" A leading question with an obvious answer: buying drugs.

The street was busy. It was a major thoroughfare with shops and public housing. A city bus discharged passengers at the next cross street.

We went up and down main streets, side streets, even alleyways for hours. She reacted to nothing. Then suddenly she recalled something. "We went down a winding road. I think we were lost."

"Did it dead-end?"

"Yeah. There was a big wall."

"I said, "What kind of"-

"I'm tired of this. Stop with the questions."

"No more. That's all."

At a little past noon, I parked the Audi and took out my phone. There were three messages. Two were commercial recordings. The other was from my ex-wife. She would want to know whether I had found Brian. I deleted the message.

I needed to check in with Novelli. "Sherrie, stay in the car. I have to make a call."

I got out and walked ahead to a fence with barbed wire evilly adorning the top.

Novelli picked up on the first ring.

"Yeah?"

"Novelli, It's me."

"Doc, tell me what's going on, then I'll catch you up."

I gave him a short rendition, staying with facts. My mind kept pushing ahead, asking him questions to find out what he knew. But he was clever, maneuvering me back to my account of events.

When I talked about Sherrie's memory of a dead end with a wooden wall, Novelli interrupted. "Dan, Dan, Dan. She's not going to cooperate, even if you give her the whole $400. She could say a particular site looked familiar, when it wasn't. I mean, just to get the money." He was lecturing me. "Dan, you *know* that. Come on, she's an addict. When she gets the cravings and feels like crap, she'll jump out of your car at a stop light. As the navy says, 'abandon Ship.'"

"Then what should I do?"

"Bring her back to her place."

"And then what?"

"Call me. I want to know you're with her."

"All right." My report ended; it was his turn.

He said, "Let's see. I've got the locations of five nests where drug bosses headquarter themselves. So there are five all-black gangs in Southwest. Four are entrenched, one a start-up. The first four stick to drugs, almost exclusively, except when low on capital. Then they steal jewelry and other valuables." There was background chatter, children arguing. He was at home with his family. Novelli said something in a stern voice, then returned to me. "Where was I? Oh yeah. The last group, we think, wants to make a name for itself. Their leader, up 'til now, has been keeping it close to the vest. But that could change overnight."

"Sal, give me their address."

"Can't do that. It's police business, and police business *only*. I will say this once, so listen. Citizens do police work once. Because they get killed."

I said, "All right, Sal. I understand what you're saying."

"That's good. Now, getting back to Sherrie. My instincts and experience with drug addicts tell me whatever she says is unreliable. But what the hell. Let me ask her some things."

I went back to the car. "Sherrie, I'm going to ask you just a few questions." Her eyes were glazed over. I placed the phone on speaker.

Sal said, "Any of the men who assaulted you have identifying marks, such as tattoos, eye patches?"

She answered, "They wore black hoodies. And green dew rags."

"How many were there?"

"Two, maybe three."

"What kind of vehicle do you remember?"

"A car was chasing us. Or maybe a truck. I don't remember what it looked like."

Novelli said, "Now, Sherrie, I want you to close your eyes. You're there in that neighborhood. At night. Look around you. What's happening?"

She moved her head from side to side, eyes open. Then closed them. "It's hot, on one side. A tall tree. Pain all over."

"Sherrie," I said, "what was hot?"

"I have no idea."

"Is Brian with you?"

"I don't see him."

Novelli said, "Anything else?"

She opened her eyes. They were fearful. "There was a man, black, tall, very wide, with bug eyes." She began crying. "He grabbed me. I thought he was going to kill me."

I said, "Anything else?"

"I can't do this anymore." She covered her ears and turned away.

Novelli instructed me to cut off the speaker. When I did, he said, "Dan, we'd better stop before she gets hysterical. Tell her she did a good job. What she gave us sounds plausible. Maybe she wasn't making it up."

8

I was encouraged by Sherrie's interview. She was regaining her memory, but was it accurate? I shared Novelli's doubts. It would all boil down to its usefulness, whether it would bring me closer to finding my son.

Almost certainly, Brian had been abducted by violent men. If he had escaped them, he would have turned up by now. If he were a captive, he was probably being beaten, maybe tortured. Perhaps in inconceivable ways. Or they had killed him.

I recalled a case I had read about in Cleveland, of a ten-year-old boy abducted by child traffickers. They kept him in the basement of a row house fortified by wrought iron bars over nailed-down windows. He was beaten with leather belts. By some highly unlikely means, he managed to open a window and squeeze between bars to freedom. He ran helter-skelter up the block in his underwear until a neighbor called the police.

I reached across to the GPS, and programmed it to scan within a five-mile radius. There were dozens of winding streets that stopped at dead ends. The system called up the name of the first street. I steered onto it, dodging potholes and passing abandoned buildings. The street ended at a factory. The other dead ends yielded nothing resembling the turnaround and wall Sherrie had mentioned.

I glanced sideways at the passenger seat. Sherrie was asleep. Her breathing was shallow and innocent, as if her body had found a sanctuary from its chemical afflictions. I came around the car, picked her up, and moved her to the backseat. She stirred, but I found a blanket in the trunk that comforted her back into sleep.

I drove her back home and put her in bed. She folded in to a protective position.

Seeing her like this, I could easily be lulled into a false sense of security. But she could awaken at any time and elope. That didn't mean I had to stay awake all night. In the closet was a fold-up chair that I propped against the bedroom door.

With great reservations, I took the thick roll of cash out of my pocket, and counted out $400 worth of twenties. I stuffed them into a white envelope, which I placed in a drawer. I would give it to Sherrie if she screamed for it.

My role, as a guard, would last only until early tomorrow morning, Saturday, when I would resume my search of the Southwest.

I called Claire. A male voice said, "Yeah?"

"Is this Billy?"

"Who are you?" He was suspicious.

"I'm Dan Davis. Your wife and I talked today, about Sherrie. Can I talk with her?"

"She's asleep."

"It's important, Billy. Can you wake her up?"

He hesitated. "Look, if it were me, I'd turn my back on Sherrie. She's already put Claire through hell." His voice rose. "More than once."

"Don't hang up, Billy. Let me ask you. If something bad happened to Drake, what would you do?"

"Nothing bad will happen to him. I'll protect him no matter what."

"Billy, my son is missing, and Claire may be able to help me."

"What's your name again?"

"Dan. Dan Davis."

"Hold on." Minutes went by.

With great relief, I heard Claire's voice. "Doctor, you found her?"

I let her know the details.

"Thank you very much. So, what are you going to do tomorrow? Look for your son?"

I told her when I was leaving Sherrie's, and she said she would be over a little before then.

"Claire, I hate to ask this, but do you know anybody who could sell me Dilaudid capsules?"

"If I did, I'd call the cops on 'em real fast."

When I opened my eyes, it was after 6 AM. The sun was not up yet.

I placed my ear on the bedroom door and heard no noise inside. Sherrie was still asleep.

It was time to clean myself up. Looking in the bathroom mirror, I noticed a sore spot on the side of my head, above the ear. It pulsed to the touch. My hair was matted and spiked, protesting its neglect. The first throes of a headache insinuated itself into consciousness.

I fumbled about and managed to take a quick and very cold shower. A hand tremor made shaving difficult.

Claire came over as I was pulling a jersey over my head. She bent down and extracted a Crock-Pot from a woven shopping bag. "I'm giving you a nice big helping of beef stew for lunch. And don't say no."

She was a good-hearted woman, almost the antithesis of her sister.

There was another bag that contained cleaning supplies. Claire placed her thumbs inside her jeans, fingers outward. She said, "Now get out of here so's I can clean this awful kitchen."

I spent the next twelve hours in the Audi looking for a dead end with a wooden wall. The only thing I found was futility. Southwest was a cruel creature feeding off my dwindling hopes.

9

It was Tuesday morning, and the phone was ringing. I picked up. Sal's voice sounded encouraging.

"Dan, it's me. We think we found the hoodie guy."

"Hey, that's great. It didn't take long."

"He fits Sherrie's description to a tee," Sal said. "We grabbed him up with a short retarded guy who called him Big Dog when we made the arrest. He put up a fight, but we got him down and cuffed him. He's at Central now."

"How can I help, Sal?"

"This is what I want you to do. Go to Sherrie's place. We need her down here for a lineup, to identify him, so we can hold this guy and interrogate him."

Elated with the news, I got myself showered, shaved, and dressed. I wasn't hungry for breakfast. After some confusion about where I had parked the Audi, I took out the remote and hit the Find button. The Audi played a bar of a familiar song, and in a few seconds, disregarding caution, I spun it out of the lot.

Before I reached Sherrie's front door, I heard the sound of blaring music. Nobody opened to my bangs. "Dammit!" Her childish self-involvement frustrated me to no end.

Sherrie said, "Go away. You weren't invited. Get lost." I could see her shirt through the bottom of the window, above the rolled-up curtain. A light-skinned black man was behind her, swaying his hips to a South American rhythm, a smile on his face.

"Sherrie, it's Dan. *Let me in.*"

There was a pause. Then a click. As I entered, she disappeared into the bedroom. I heard most of what she said. She couldn't find money in her purse. "Shit! Where is it, Derek?"

She hadn't found the envelope containing $400, not yet.

Reappearing in the living room, she confronted the man. "The hundred dollars. You stole it, didn't you?"

The man said, "That's not true, Sherrie. I just got here, and I've been in this room the whole time."

She shouted, "Fuck! What's happening to me!" This was followed by jibberish as if she were creating new words with every syllable. She moved her head back and forth, as if trying to shake something loose. "*Get away!*" She dropped down on the floor, on all fours, back straight. One hand moved in a circular motion as if searching for a small object. Then, as if on its own, the hand moved backwards, where it grasped her jeans at the calves. The other hand suddenly appeared in front of her face. She rubbed it against both cheeks, then looked curiously at it, as if trying to determine if it actually existed. Wondering what was going on, I walked over to the black man.

"What did she take?" He looked away, unresponsive. My temper was rising. I grabbed him by the collar and shouted, "Tell me what you sold her!" There was a tremor in his cheek. I said, "If you don't, I'm calling the cops."

He took something out of his pocket and opened his palm. It was a circular gray pill. Ecstasy. A mood elevator, but it was often mixed with other drugs like PCP that caused hallucinations.

I could hardly contain myself. "Goddamn it. Look what you've done to her. Get out of this house. *Now.*" He left and slammed the door.

I sat on a rickety chair, trying to calm down and deal with the insanity of the situation. Tears of frustration came, but I didn't cry.

She was emitting an animal-like sound. I bent down by her side.

"Sherrie, this is what happened. You took something bad that makes you see things that aren't real. Hang in there, and you'll be okay soon." That may not have been true. I didn't know how much she had taken, or when.

She made no response, obviously fixated on frightening visions.

I let a few minutes go by until the animal sounds stopped.

"Sherrie, it's Dan, Brian's father. Let me ask you, when did you take the pills?"

"What does it matter? Let me die." She was suicidally depressed.

"You need lots of water and wet towels. I'll be back in a very short while."

When I came back, she had found a teddy bear and was holding it tightly. I convinced her to drink some water. She was at risk for water depletion. The towels seemed to comfort her as much as the bear. There was a mild but nearly continuous tremor in her arms and hands. I started to worry about seizure activity.

There was no choice but to wait it out. Several hours went by. She started to cycle between wake and sleep. I kept pouring water down her throat in very small doses.

In my restlessness, I made some cruddy coffee, black and cold, and drank it in the kitchen. I brought the mug out to Sherrie after filling it with water.

I tried to test her orientation and memory, but it was not possible. She mouthed answers slowly, without speaking.

With eyes suddenly wide open, she spied the mug. "Coffee. Coffee." Her intonation was of a child. She gestured as if drinking.

I ran to the kitchen. She craved caffeine, and lots of it. It could sharpen her senses and bring her back to reality. Strong black coffee would be best. I sat her up, and she sipped eagerly, as if it were a healing elixir.

She rose up from the floor and lay on the couch. Some color returned to her face.

Soon she took a shower and dressed appropriately in street clothing.

She was docile. "What do I do now? I feel like I'm here but not here."

I asked her to walk back and forth, wall to wall. She swayed, but her balance was adequate. At the third try, she leaned against the window sill. "My back hurts. It always hurts." One of the keys to pain control was to deflect the mind away from it. I told her to sit down and watch me while I moved about in Tai Chi fashion.

A question occurred to me. Should I give her two over-the-counter pain pills? Given the level of pain she was experiencing, and the aftereffects of the drug she had taken, I decided not to.

Before we left, Novelli called. Big Dog was saying nothing. But he hadn't demanded a lawyer yet. He would stay in a locked room with a one way mirror. They had charged him with assault.

When we left the house, Sherrie asked where we were going. I told her. She refused to get in my car. After several attempts at persuasion, I stood on the passenger side, door opened.

She hesitated, then put her head down and slid across the seat. In 15 minutes, we drove into the police headquarter's lot.

10

At the top of the station house stairs, I spotted Novelli. He waved, then motioned for me to talk with him in private. I found a bench and explained to Sherrie that I would be right back.

Novelli said, "Do you really think she can do this? She looks like she just came out of a grave."

I said, "She's scared, Sal. But she'll let me help her. I'm going to stay close. The worst case scenario is that she sees that gang member again."

He sighed. "We'll need rosary beads on this one. All the divine intervention we can get."

I rejoined Sherrie, smiling confidently. It didn't help.

Her hands were in half-fists, arms against her face. She said, "This place, I hate it. The last time I was here, they treated me like shit. Get me in and out as fast as you can."

Novelli moved us through security. We walked down a narrow corridor filled with people. There were red arrows on the walls directing pedestrians to police units I had never heard of.

A tall thin middle-aged woman in a navy suit ushered us into a small room. "The detective told me about your situation, Ms. McClintock. I'm sorry you have to go through this. The district attorney's office thanks you very much for helping to arrest and convict people who think they can hold our city hostage to their violence."

Sherrie focused her narrowed gaze on the attorney. "Who are you?"

"ADA Sterman. Let me tell you the drill." She was hurrying her speech, not a good tactic here.

Sherrie interrupted her. "Look, I really don't care about the drill. Where do I stare out at the men in the lineup?"

"First you have to write a statement as to what happened to you when this man assaulted you."

Sherrie let out a moan and cradled her head in her arm. Looking back at me, she said, "Why did you take me here?"

"You know why. My son, Brian."

I turned to face Sterman, speaking in muted fashion. "Can I help her write it?"

She directed a strained expression toward me while mulling over the request.

"Is she learning disabled, illiterate?"

I turned to Sherrie. "How far did you get in school?"

"Eleventh grade."

"Did a school psychologist administer some tests to measure your behavior?"

"I remember a teacher wearing those tiny reading glasses. There were inkblots, math, some other stuff."

"Okay, Sherrie, what about your performance in English class? Were you able to write?"

"No. I got help, but it didn't do any good. I can't put two ideas together on paper. And reading? People order for me at restaurants." Her face opened up with a clear memory. "Like Brian did when you bought us dinner."

I was encouraged. "Yes. I saw him do that for you." I turned to face the prosecutor.

"Ms. Sterman, I am a licensed psychologist in this state. In my opinion, Sherrie McClintock has at least two language-based learning deficits." It sounded legitimate, so I said it.

She steepled her fingers, thumbs crossed. "All right, we'll go with that." She pointed to her phone. "I have to take a break. When I'm gone, I want the two of you to write an account of what happened." She looked about, but there was no writing pad. "Better yet, Doctor, create a file in that computer on the table, leaving nothing out. When I get back, I'll overview it. Sherrie, tell the doctor everything you recall."

Soon after Sterman left, I smiled at Sherrie. "We're a team. You don't have to worry." I wanted to relax her into the task ahead. It would not be easy.

She lost concentration several times. We took breaks, and she was able to regain focus. My clarifying questions filled in some gaps.

Sterman came back and went over it, circling phrases she thought needed changing. I could tell she was a perfectionist, the kind of person who would never be satisfied with another's work. Finally, after the third draft, she asked for the document to be printed out. She proofread it one more time. "This will have to do, Doctor." She pointed for us to leave the room.

Coming up behind us, she said, "The lineup is forming in the room two doors to the right." We entered the next room. Sterman pointed at me. "Stand over on Sherrie's left side." This maneuver was to prevent Sherrie from seeing any of the suspects as they walked down the hall.

Sterman took a key and unlocked the door. There was only one light switch that jolted the bank of ceiling lights awake. We sat down in stackable plastic chairs. Out of the corner of my eye, I saw Sherrie start to shake like a frightened addict that she was. Sterman asked her, "Can you do this, Sherrie?" There was no response.

Sterman looked at me blankly. "Dr. Davis, she cannot be impaired in any way while she observes the lineup. Is that clear?"

"Perfectly. Give us a couple of minutes."

At this point, Sherrie's distress was worsened more by anxiety than the drugs she had taken. Her eyes darted about, like a rabbit looking for an owl. She smelled a foul odor I smelled too. The odor of countless lost souls, victims of violent men and women, passing through this way station of despair.

I said, "Sherrie, I'm going to calm you down." She appeared as fragile as a china doll. I leaned my upper body toward hers. She whimpered as I moved my arms and hands along her shoulders. The whimper turned into a moan. Then the dam burst as she held her hands over her eyes. She cried in rolling, rocking sobs.

Sterman looked away at the floor. She was obviously uncomfortable with Sherrie's outburst.

She quieted herself by taking deep breaths.

Sterman coughed, cleared her throat, and said, "Sherrie, as you see the men in the room, remember, they can't see you. Also, I will be with you the whole time. There's nothing to be afraid of."

Sterman consulted her cell phone. "The men will soon come in through that door, single file."

There was the sound of shoes on floor as the men filed in. Six hefty African American men turned to face the window. All wore black hoodies. Sterman asked Sherrie to take her time, look at each man, and see if she had a clear recognition of any.

Sherrie's eyes moved down the row, studying each man, then looked away. Showing no emotion, she said, "I don't recognize any of them."

Later, Novelli called. Big Dog was saying nothing. For the next few hours, he would stay in a locked room. The assault charge was still in force. If in another few hours there was no tangible evidence against him, he could leave.

I wanted to be of some potential assistance to the investigation. Perhaps Big Dog would slip, and I could use his statement to reveal something about Brian's disappearance. Novelli allowed me into the observation room.

11

Novelli began. "Just who are you?"

"I tol' you. Name's Big Dog."

"I mean your given name."

"It *is* my given name. My mom named me. I was a big kid. And real strong."

He grinned broadly. "Used it to fight dudes on the street. Anybody who'd take me on." His bulging eyes fixed on Novelli as he moved his index finger back and forth in admonishing fashion. "You white folks don't know this, fightin' makes you stronger. Better than eatin' Wheaties."

There was fearlessness in his demeanor. He was ridiculing us. Nevertheless, for some reason, I found him likeable.

Novelli said, "Were you raised in Baltimore?"

"Must have. It's the only place I know."

"You still live here?"

"Yeah. But I move around a lot. A while back I moved into a red house on the end of some block."

"What's the name of the street?"

"Do I look like a map to you?"

"You mean you can't read?"

My thoughts turned to Big Dog's photo and fingerprints, whether the NCIC had them stored. Obviously, something tangible had to turn up.

A uniformed cop entered the room and silently motioned for Novelli to accompany him. Novelli looked to me. He said, "You can come too, Dan. But only to listen."

Big Dog said, "Ah, man, let's get this over with."

In the hallway, Novelli explained my presence to the uniformed officer. The cop said, "I get it. But this is why I found you." He handed a stack of papers to Novelli.

He said, "Novelli, I can't ever remember this happening. It's downright strange."

"What's strange, Kalecki?"

"The thing is, I can't find any records on this Big Dog person. We ran his prints, photoed his face. There's no arrest record, not even a drunken disorderly. Never went to school or got a driver's license or owned a car. In fact, he was never born. No birth certificate. There's absolutely nothing. Like he just sprouted up out of the ground."

Novelli said, "There's got to be an answer. Maybe he's from Canada. Or Mexico."

"Not likely, in my opinion. I went over the tape of his first interview. He has the speech cadence and vocabulary of a black male from an East Coast city. Most likely from here, Philly, or New York."

Novelli growled, "So we have no concrete information on him, he's not giving us anything useful, but we suspect he's from the East Coast. In other words, we've got nothing."

Kalecki rubbed his beard. "I do recall we had a Jane Doe about twelve years ago, a homeless woman. She came down from New York looking for someone. Late one night, on Lombard, she was hit over the head repeatedly with a brick. She didn't survive the trip to UMAB Hospital."

"How did you know she came from New York?"

"We didn't know for two years. They listed her as a Jane Doe until Ben looked through her clothes. There was a label on her dress from a New York thrift store."

Novelli was tired. "So what does that case have to do with this one?"

"As far as the NYPD was concerned, she never existed. No paper, no nothing. Everywhere, in every state, they came up with nothing."

"I'm tired, Kalecki. Let's get back to the present. We had him strip. There were no distinguishing characteristics on his body or his clothes. He has that eye condition called exophthalmia, or bulging eyes, but we don't know if an ophthalmologist examined it."

Novelli collected himself. "Okay, I'm going to assume, for argument's sake, that he lived in Baltimore, moved about a lot, for most of his life."

Kalecki said, "Why don't you put somebody on his tail, follow him to where he lives?"

"We're going to release him at 11 tonight. What are the chances we'll be able to tail him in the dark? He'll know we're behind him, and he'll know the best places to hide along his way.

I said, "Sal, I'll follow him. Let me do this."

"I can't, Dan. Come on, you're a civilian. Where he lives is a place you don't want to go. Besides, it would break every cop rule in the book."

He was right. But right gave me no hope, only blind alleys.

The unproductive interview was one event in a string of failures that left me feeling that I was in a room of trick mirrors and ghosts.

12

I was out continuing my search when Novelli called. He said, "We have some stuff that could belong to your son. There might be something you'd recognize."

Taken off guard, I replied, "Where did you find it?"

"Look, my friend, all I will say is, we came in through the bathroom window. Case closed."

"Do you think he was there? Alive?"

"I'm not sure, Dan. But if you get over here, you can draw us closer. Come over to the station house, right now."

The place didn't reek of cigar smoke. This time it was fried chicken. Big boxes of it. On three circular fold-up tables.

Novelli offered me a plate and a plastic fork. He was in a celebratory mood. "It took two uniforms to haul all this food. It's the best, and plenty to go around. Eat it and weep." After sipping from a Coke cup, he turned to his side and pointed downward. In front of a locker was a white trash bag. He told me to put on a pair of plastic gloves. "Now empty everything, one at a time, into that tray." He pointed to a wide tray with a deep bottom. "Eyeball each item, and set aside ones you think in any way are related to Brian."

There was a thick hemp rope, a shorter rope, an unopened roll of paper towels, a Swiss army knife, two cans of off-brand beer, $30 cash, and a red-and-white box of Marlboros, empty. The last item struck a chord. I recalled the restaurant manager in Ocean City. He saw Brian carrying the same kind of pack. I conferred with Novelli. He picked it up with a pair of tweezers and dropped it into a small evidence bag.

He said, "Now we're getting somewhere. I'll take it to fingerprinting."

"Sal, what are they going to compare the print with?"

He smiled. "You're a clever guy. That's where you come in. Go home and bring us a print of Brian's, preferably on a glass or plastic cup."

I was excited. "I'll be at the lab early in the morning."

13

I took the Beltway West and beat a backup by driving the shoulder. Motorists beeped their dissatisfaction and flashed me the bird, but it didn't matter. This was a minor crime at best. My son was missing, so I didn't much care if I were pulled over.

As I approached my house, all I thought about was turning the key in the front door and finding something the police could use.

In the house, thirst overcame me. I headed for the fridge and found two lonely looking bottles of Bass Ale. I gulped them down, nearly without stopping.

Moving to the rear window, I stared out at the floodlights.

Something made me push the palm of my hand into contact with the window. I saw a smudge and visualized Brian drinking at the dining room table with his favorite glass mug. He used to carry it back to his room. I remembered because Molly told him to keep it in the kitchen.

I hurried into his room, banging my arm against the door frame.

There was a ceramic mug on the window sill. I picked it up by its base with a tissue, and held it to the ceiling light. Along the side, I could make out what appeared to be a smudge with ridges. Very carefully, I lowered the mug into a small box, and stabilized it with paper towels.

I thought of driving back to the police lab, but it was late. At this hour, the crime lab was being cleaned.

I spent a nearly sleepless night in my own bed.

Novelli's call woke me as rays of morning light filtered through the sheer curtains. He told me to bring the sample down to Central, to a tech whose work he respected.

Traffic was merciful, and I parked at the police station before eight.

I saw her nameplate and waved. Sandy, wearing tight orange gloves, shook my hand. She took the box. "So you're the unfortunate soul who's fallen in with Novelli." She had a remarkable smile that radiated to sparkling eyes.

Her uniform was utterly white like the ice cream man of my childhood. Flaming Irish red hair was combed back in a ponytail. She spoke with a working-class accent.

"Dr. Davis, we have a rule, a kind of hidden one, which is, crimes involving Baltimore residents take priority. But we do make exceptions. I used to live in Montgomery County. Wish I still did." I assumed she enjoyed the woods and parks that Baltimore lacked.

Her movements were quick and precise. Turning to an adjacent table, she held up the mug to an intense light. "Ah, yes, there's the culprit. It's very distinctive." She moved to another table and maneuvered its contents. The mug and the cigarette box were next to each other on an aluminum platter. Taking a small brush, she powdered the print on the mug. Four finger ridges materialized. She scanned the images, and they appeared clearly on the left side of the screen. It was a precise art.

Next, she repeated the same procedure with the prints on the cigarette box. In a few seconds, the prints appeared on the right side of the screen. Above and in the middle, the word "MATCH" pulsated in red.

Sandy smiled and said, "I'll send the findings to the detective squad, Doctor. So glad to be of help."

I smiled broadly. She smiled back. A match.

14

Late that evening, Novelli and Kalecki came to my motel room. I was anxious to talk with them, to find out whether either had made a breakthrough.

I sat at a cheap formica-topped desk while the two men stood.

Novelli began. "This isn't a big deal, Dan." He scratched his head, obviously trying to be tactful. I braced. "After our initial search of the premises, we still suspected Brian was in the house, hidden away somewhere. So we applied for a search warrant. The judge, however, won't issue it. He found out about our unauthorized raid, and that Brian wasn't found."

Kalecki stared at a landscape above the bed. Hands tautly at his sides, he seemed to be trying to become invisible.

Novelli continued. "The wild card in all this, Dan, is Capo has a lawyer. He went to the district attorney and told her about the 'home invasion,' as he put it."

Kalecki intervened. "Sorry, Dan. I know you must be frustrated. Before we went in, it's possible a drug mule saw us coming and alerted gang members in the house. They must have had time to take Brian away. Where to, at this time, I do not know." It sounded like a long shot, so I filed it under Highly Unlikely Scenario.

I said, "Could there be an informant on the force?"

Novelli replied, "Dan, something like that would happen once in a blue moon. Forget that line of thought."

I grasped at straws. "What do we do now? By going into the house, you took a calculated risk." I paused while thinking of what to say and how to say it.

I did not want to alienate them by questioning what they had done. "I think you did the right thing. You had to act quickly. Brian could have been in grave danger. For your efforts, I thank you both."

Novelli looked relieved. "No problem, Dan."

I said, "Can the police department apply again for a search warrant?"

"We could," Kalecki replied. "But now we have this ruling, I wouldn't bet on an overturn."

"Then for now our options have run out," I said.

Novelli was upbeat. "For now they have, Dan. But don't worry. We'll think of something."

They let themselves out while I reviewed what they had said. There was nothing even remotely encouraging.

My head slumped to the table while my mind fell into a black hole.

I lifted myself up and found a bottle of Wild Turkey and a paper cup.

15

I drove west, along Fayette Street, and pulled up to the curb when I reached Schuyler in the heart of Southwest Baltimore. Once again, I programmed the GPS to take me to streets that dead-ended.

The first six were failures. I was losing focus and hope.

The next candidate was a serpentine road called Coulter Street. It straightened out as it passed a school then wound up a sloping hill. Having lost attention, I almost turned off the road at a fork.

Houses were not dilapidated here. I saw home owners doing yard work in their front yards, talking to each other over low rustic fences.

Up ahead was a sharp turn sign. I braked and descended into a turnaround like the ones I had seen as a child, at the end of a trolley line. It was almost perfectly round, with three houses on its perimeter. There were hedges and flower gardens on each side of paved driveways. It had the order and symmetry common to suburbia.

There it was. At the far side of the arc stood a wooden wall. About twelve feet high, perhaps fourteen feet long, of stacked wooden planks painted a faded yellow. There were several deep horizontal cut marks a few feet above the base. Perhaps from car bumpers that impacted the wall.

I looked about. Some fifteen feet from the wall, on the street, was a large burn mark. Its rectangular shape was about the length and width of a compact car. The size of my son's vehicle.

I took photos of the wall and the black spot.

Not knowing what to do next, I sat on a rock, hoping an idea would crystallize.

There was a man, perhaps in his fifties, coming toward me, walking briskly. He was wearing a white sweater, brown slacks, and loafers. His gait and dress conveyed both affluence and anxiety.

"You there. Who are you?"

He could be anybody. We were strangers, and he had me on the defensive.

I said, "I'm an insurance investigator. Name's Crowley."

"What is it that you want?"

"I'm here to photograph a car in a crash. But, obviously, it's not here." I smiled, hoping he saw truth in my words. He watched me with a fixed stare. I said, "Just this mark on the road, probably from vehicle immolation."

The man rubbed a hand across his chin. He said, "It happened four days ago. Late, after eleven I'm sure. There was a sudden flash of light. I looked out from my upstairs window. There was a huge funneling flame shooting up from the road here. I thought somebody had thrown gasoline all over a car."

I said, "God, I hope nobody was in the vehicle when it went up."

"That's exactly what I thought. I prayed there was not."

He was becoming less suspicious and more agreeable. His eyes softened when he said, "Listen, it's getting chilly out here. I'd better go inside. Why don't you come in and have a nice cup of hot chocolate? We could share some more ideas about this incident. By the way, my name is Rufus Johnson." He reached out his hand, and I shook it.

I said, "No, Rufus, I really have to be going."

"Oh, it won't be long. I'm very interested in what more you have to say about this. Honestly, I haven't had an involved conversation in a long time. My wife doesn't talk much."

Something about him seemed off. Maybe it was the beseeching tonal quality of his speech.

We walked together toward his house as raindrops started to pepper my jacket.

In the kitchen, we sat down around a sturdy maple table, talking casually. He was hospitable and gracious. Knowing I could leave and return to the search had a palliative effect, but the lies I told him played upon my conscience. I had to dispel them.

"Rufus, I need to confess something. I told you some untruths. My name is Dan, Dan Davis. I'm not an insurance investigator. I'm a psychologist."

He became irate, pounding his fist on the table, causing his cup to fall onto the floor. He bellowed, "Here I trusted you at your word, and you lied to me. Tell me, why would you do such a thing?"

His moods appeared unstable. Bipolar came to mind.

I said, "I'm sorry. I'll go." I got up and turned to leave. He said nothing.

A third voice came from behind. "Rufus, settle down."

His wife was in a motorized wheelchair. She was wearing a red wig, wavy and youngish. Her voice was weak. I could hear her breathing. "Tell me, dear, what were you two talking about?"

Rufus waved her off. "We just had a misunderstanding, Belle."

"What is your friend's name?"

"We were getting to that when you came in. I think he said it is Dan Crowley Davis." He stared at me.

Belle said, "Please, Mr. Davis, sit down." I complied.

She continued. "You look so troubled. Tell me about it."

I had an urge to flee because of all the questions that lay ahead. Experience informed me that people with movement restrictions prized social interaction. I could foresee an extended conversation with Belle, one I wanted to avoid. My search was going to continue, and as soon as possible.

In truncated manner, I told them about the events that had brought me to their street. "I think that black mark out there was where my son's car caught fire. That's why I was out there. I don't think he was in the burning car. He may have been dragged out by gang members. What I don't understand is what happened to the car. Do you think it was towed?"

Rufus said, "Because I suspected gang activity, I stayed away. This is ordinarily a quiet community, but there have been recent incidents that were probably gang-related. I keep a kind of lookout for unusual developments."

He pointed across the yard where the other houses stood. "My two neighbors don't know or care about what I'm doing. They are elderly and rarely leave their houses.

I asked him, "Did you see a tow truck out there?"

"No, I didn't." From his eyes I could see there was something on his mind. "I apologize, Dan, for my harsh words. Now that I know what is happening to you, I can understand why you said what you did."

He turned to his wife. "You know, Belle, something just occurred to me. Remember when your brother closed down his shop and went to work for the newspaper?"

"I do. The last I heard, Dexter's retiring at the end of this year."

Rufus snapped a finger. "Then he's still there. I'm going to call him." He went into another room. There was the click of a landline pickup.

Looking about the kitchen, I noticed at least a dozen antique radios, all encased in wood, with vertical grills where the sound emerged. Each was clearly visible on a wide display table.

Belle said, "I see you have your eyes on Rufus's radio collection. Each is tuned precisely to a particular station that plays jazz, classical, blues, all news, politics, and a few others. He turns a radio on depending upon his mood. The man would be lost without his cherished toys. They make him feel like he has more control over his life since he had to retire on disability."

Rufus returned with a smile. He pointed at me and signaled that I should accompany him into the other room. "I'm talking with Dexter, Dan." He handed the phone to me.

We exchanged greetings. I asked if he thought he could help me.

"Well, let's start where you are right now. Less than three miles southeast from Belle's, at the edge of Southwest, lives a bad bunch of punks. It's a street gang that's less than a year old. The boss's name is Anthony Carstens, nickname Capo. Let's see, house purchase is a matter of public record. I'll call you back."

I rejoined Rufus and Belle for further conversation and coffee. About an hour later, the phone rang. It was Dexter. He told me, "It's 4525 Schofield, near the Railroad Museum."

His voice took on an anxious quality. "Listen, Dr. Davis, don't go near that place. They are highly unfriendly."

"What do you mean?"

"The police believe they're responsible for three murders. That's one every four months. They're off to a good start, wouldn't you say?"

After thanking Rufus, I bid them good-bye and headed back to Southwest.

When I found Schofield, I parked one block from the Nest, under a tall poplar.

Novelli warned me not to play police. But if I called him, what would happen? He would tell me to leave. But they would take no action without a warrant. If they could secure one, would they mishandle the situation and overreact? In a standoff, would the captors kill Brian?

I had to do something. I was one step ahead of an unknown reckoning.

Once out of my car, I would be in no man's land.

Doubts unsettled my mind like a bouncing ball on a roulette wheel. I had to block them out. Finding my son was all that mattered.

That would take action. Not ideas.

16

I got out of the Audi and headed up the sidewalk. An old man walked in my direction. He stared at me and uttered some incomprehensible words. As I passed him, he scowled. From behind me, I heard, "Go back to the suburbs where you belong, whitey." I kept walking until I reached 4525. It was a typical cottage, one story, wood frame.

There were two large men standing on the porch. They walked down the steps and stopped within six feet of me. Their arms were crossed, and a smug sort of anger showed on their faces. They had to be Capo's enforcers, barring the trespasser.

One of the men said, "Who the fuck are you?" I said nothing, only looked him in the eye. The other one smiled. "He must be crazy. A cracker in a nasty black neighborhood."

I said, "Where is my son?"

"You think I know or care where your son's at?" Both chuckled. "What you want, a knife in your heart, or bullet in your head?"

He advanced until his face was less than a foot from mine.

Reaching for as calm a voice as possible, I said, "Give me Brian Davis. Now." I pointed toward the house. "Or I go in there to talk to your boss."

In a loud voice, the man on my right said, "Fuck you! You come here acting like you own the world." He was seething. "You don't own *shit.* Now get out of here, before you *can't* walk out." We stared each other down.

A tall thin neatly dressed man came down from the porch and approached us. He could have been a model for men's clothing, wearing a sleek suit, exuding confidence. His past and reputation were not foreign to me. I had read an article about him in a magazine. The author viewed him as an astute inner-city businessman with "connections" to the drug trade.

An enforcer faced around at him. "Capo, we got this under control."

Capo pointed to the other one. "Tony, come here." They huddled together like football players, talking in whispers. There were muffled words. Then Capo clapped his hands.

They came toward me and stopped, an enforcer on each side of me. Capo was in front. He said, "What makes you think this guy is in my place?" The tone of his voice sounded calm, reasoned.

I said, "I know where he is."

An extended silence ensued. He lit a cigarette and blew smoke in my face. "So, are you going all over these neighborhoods trying to point the finger wherever you want?" He moved back. I showed defiance.

"Tony, give him just a sample of what we do to people like him."

Tony reared back with his right arm while I braced for the blow. It came with full force into my chest. A throbbing pain radiated from the point of impact. My knees buckled, but I resisted going to the ground.

I felt a fist crash into my jaw. My head snapped back, eyes open, but all I saw on the way down was a cloudy and very brief video of people pointing at me and laughing.

The back of my head hit the pavement, and I was gone.

When I came to, Capo's face was next to mine.

He said, "You see how heroes feel when they're hit so hard it knocks them out?"

I took some deep breaths and slowly went up on all fours. It was a mixture of fear and anger in my voice. "The cops won't like this. They know exactly where I am."

Capo said, "Then why aren't they here? The last time I saw them in this neighborhood, they were eating donuts up on Addison Street."

He pointed at one of his enforcers and motioned a hand toward me. "Come over here, Bo. Take his cell."

The other one said, "I'll bet you ten bucks, Bo, it's in his jacket pocket."

I moved backward, but it was too late. He grabbed it roughly. After looking it over, he said to his accomplice, "Hey homey, this is a good phone. Got all these apps. The internet, I can get O's tickets." He smiled widely at me.

Capo said, "Go inside and take it with you." Bo left.

"Now, Tony, lift his wallet." He turned me to one side and rifled the wallet out of my pants. Capo said, "Give it to me." He inspected each item and placed my driver's license and a business card in his shirt pocket. It contained my phone number, fax, and e-mail address. "Get rid of the wallet and everything in it."

He removed the license from his shirt and studied it. "Here's what you're going to do, Dr. Dan. Go home and get some rest. Then stay in your nice little house, and keep your nose out of my business."

17

I dragged myself to the Audi, feeling as if I was carrying a dead weight on my back.

Once in the seat, I inserted the key. Driving in labored fashion, I found a park, where the Audi found refuge behind benches.

Nausea engulfed me, and I put my head out the door and vomited. There were some strands of blood, but not enough to indicate a substantial amount of internal bleeding into my digestive tract.

I turned the rear view mirror until I was staring straight into it. The left side of my jaw and cheek above it were bruised purple. I felt along the jawbone. It was painful but not broken. That was a relief. On the cheek, there was swelling of the muscle tissue, but no skin tear.

Reclining the seat, I lifted up my shirt and probed my chest. There was tenderness along three bruised ribs, and a numb pain that would probably be quelled by over-the-counter pain relievers.

I drove east and found Pratt Street in the downtown direction. On the right, coming up was a chain pharmacy. It was busy, but I found a parking space.

As I walked inside past the automatic doors, I heard, "Would you like a free sample, sir?" It was an employee, a young black woman in thick glasses. I turned toward her. She said, "Ooo, that's bad!"

When I reached the analgesics, it occurred to me that I had a full bottle of pain relieving gel caps in my motel room. That meant that all I needed was a yellow concealer to cover the purple bruise. It was in stock. I paid for it and went back to the hotel room to shower and minister to my body.

18

After a fitful sleep, I dressed and went to the front desk. They provided me with the location of a phone store. It was down the street a few blocks in the Inner Harbor.

They reprogrammed the new I phone and installed useful apps. The stolen cell was deactivated after messages were downloaded.

There were four e-mails and one voice mail. I scrolled to the voice message. It was Capo.

"Hey, Dr. Davis, are you doing all right? I sure hope so.

"The situation is the same. We have your package.

"On Monday, April 7, at 7 PM, I want fifty thousand dollars dropped off on Schroeder between Durbin and Ulysses. Give it to me all in twenties, wrapped in rubber bands. Put it in a new blue suitcase. Place the suitcase in the trash bin, on the mailbox side of the street.

"No cops. Repeat, no cops. Any hint of police presence, and you know what will happen.

"After we get paid, I will call your office number. If you follow these instructions, there will be no problem."

A click indicated Capo had hung up.

19

Claire provided me with Webb's address. He lived so close to Johns Hopkins Hospital I could see one of its smokestacks from his front steps. In the air was a scent of burning chemicals. Black soot coated the top of the nearest chimney.

Webb answered my knock. "Come on in, Doc. There's plenty of room for you. The place is a lot bigger than it looks from the outside."

He showed me into the living room. The furniture was simple and comfortable. I chose a colonial rocker, favoring the motion it afforded, metaphorical to the restless feeling I couldn't quell.

Webb started out. "How is Sherrie doing, Doc?"

"She's better now. But what concerns me is that she may have pills hidden somewhere in her house, and enough money to buy plenty more."

Webb said, "That is one bad addiction. She tried going through rehab twice. It didn't do any good. I mean, she got clean, but only for a few weeks."

"Webb, for all the good that pain medicine does, they also make the patient walk the line. What do you do with the dosage when the pain increases? How much do you raise it? If the pain stabilizes, do you cut the dose, or keep it at the same level?"

He said, "Spending time with Sherrie, you must be wondering if Brian took some pills with her."

"I think it's unlikely, Webb. He doesn't use the kind of drugs she takes. He favors mainstream ones, like alcohol and marijuana. I'm almost certain of that."

There was a lull in the conversation. I thought about why I was here.

Webb tapped hands against his leg, supplying percussion to a silent song. He was a laid-back likeable man and a devoted friend who cared about desperate people like Sherrie. He lived by a few principles and winged the rest.

On the way to the bathroom, I went to the kitchen and glanced out at a well-trimmed lawn. Webb's mother was aging, but the garden and lawn were well tended. They had Webb's stamp on them.

In a raised brick-bordered garden, sprouted fall plants with yellow and purple flowers. Beyond the garden was a metal pole on which a chained motorcycle leaned.

I pointed to it. "Is it one of the heavier weights?"

Webb replied, "Sure is. That's my baby. Nothing like it when you hit the open road, when I really air it out. That first ride after the winter storage reminds you of what you been missing all winter. You ever had one?"

"No, Webb. When I was young, we favored the muscle cars, like the Plymouth Duster."

"Oh yeah. That TV show. *Dukes of Hazzard*."

"It had a formula for every episode. But even though you knew what was going to happen, it was fun because you got to see your favorite cars every week."

Webb grabbed a beer and asked me if I wanted one. I declined. He pointed to the front of the house. "Let's sit on the porch and watch life go by."

I was aching to talk to him about Brian. "Webb, I need to tell you about something."

"Fire away, Doc."

First I told him about the search for my son. About Big Dog, Capo, the police, their invasion of the gang's residence, my meeting with Capo and his enforcers.

"The cops have helped, but they've run up against a legal wall. They made an illegal search and didn't find Brian." Anger rose up to sharpen my voice. "Hoping for a warrant, they talked to a judge, but he stonewalled it, possibly at the expense of my son's life."

He said, "Won't be the first time the system acted with no heart."

"I know, Webb, my son *must* be in there. Where else could he be? They could be keeping him behind wood paneling, or in the crawl space below the house. Meanwhile, I feel useless. The police want me to stay on the sidelines. But this waiting, I can't stand the thought that Brian might be in there, not able to move, being tortured."

Webb said, "Can you afford a couple of private cops?"

"I could hire somebody who knows the city. But are they willing to work day and night until this is resolved?"

"Yeah, and even if they get into the house and found Brian, how could they get him out with a swarm of bangers around?"

"Exactly. You know, working together, you and I might be able to do something, make some progress somehow."

"I don't know enough about this sort of thing, Doc." He stared down at the porch floor.

I said, "I see what you're saying."

"Look. You and me are friends." He leaned forward and looked right at me. "Doc, I know a lot about drug gangs, that they're cutthroat. Me and my friends, we talk about it, make stupid jokes. But the less I know about the real stuff that gangs do, the better."

He was telling me the task was out of his league. Drug gangs played by their own rules, including take no prisoners.

My heart sank. I needed his help. Who else was there?

He turned and looked at me, eyes showing sympathy. Tapping my leg, he said, "I'll tell you what. If Billy decides to throw in, I will too."

20

I said, "No. I can't use him. People with PTSD are very unpredictable, especially in a high-stress situation. They can relive combat situations and injure their own people."

Webb said, "All I ask is, talk with him. Maybe he's not as bad off as you think."

I assessed my options. What if he was right? I wanted with all my being to believe he was.

"Webb, go ahead and take me to him. I'll see what he has to say. But please understand, I'm not likely to change my mind."

I sat down on the rear seat of Webb's cycle. He drove under control, but the engine was loud, especially when Webb gunned it.

We drove over tall hills and verdant valleys, comforting in their familiarity. It was the same landscape of my youth.

Coming into view, on the right side of the road, stood an ancient farmhouse. An old man on his tractor was slowly negotiating a turn at the crest of his land. He wore a straw hat, held in place by a red bandanna, against the swirling wind. Looking at him made me think that time moved slower out here than in the city. I could have passed this place seventy years ago and seen almost exactly what I saw now. The thought relaxed me.

A few miles farther was a crescent-shaped clearing by our side of the road. Webb eased the machine into it and stopped. He angled the front tire to one side, and I dismounted. As he removed his helmet, he said, "It's probably best for you to go into the woods there alone. I don't want to be in the way."

The trail wound around stunted pine trees and clumps of junipers. It narrowed and disappeared a few times, as if trying to prevent hikers from finding their way.

Gradually, I became aware of a cliff and an unfamiliar sound.

The trail straightened, and I could look beyond, where a waterfall came into view, about twenty-five feet from top to bottom.

Billy was sitting at the cliff's edge, staring at the water as it plunged downward into an oblong pool. He didn't see me as I sat down next to him.

I cupped my hands in front of my mouth and yelled, "Billy, it's me, Dan Davis. Remember, Brian's dad?"

He seemed to come out of a trance. "Why are you here?"

"Webb gave me a ride. He thought we should talk about something."

"Why talk with me about it?"

"I'm not sure, Billy."

He looked at me like I was hollow. "Say what's on your mind, or don't say nothin' at all. I don't like when people beat around the bush."

"I have to do whatever it takes to get my son home."

"How many people gonna help you?"

"Right now, just Webb. I mean, he'll be part of this if you come aboard too."

"How many you goin' up against?"

"At least three, Billy."

"This boy of yours, why you think he's in a bad place?"

"I'm almost certain they have him in Southwest."

He looked down at the falling water as if it held a secret that would reveal itself to him if he kept his eyes on it. Sky blue eyes that had seen too much.

I said, "Billy, listen, I know about the problems you have to deal with after Iraq. I'm not putting any pressure on you."

After several minutes he said, "I've been out of work for over two years. People look at me, they can tell I'm not a regular person. When I see that look, it makes me feel like nothin'."

I said, "With your military background, you could be a big help. As an advisor, I mean."

"No, you don't understand. People tiptoe around me like I'm going to explode. Family, friends. They're afraid to let me make a decision. To be part of something important. You're the first one who did. I need that, to start over again. It's the only way."

I said, "Then we'll do it."

He said, "Yeah, but not as an advisor. You need combatants."

I tried with all my powers to read him. It was not possible. His expression was blank.

This was the kind of decision I was unaccustomed to make, one that forfeited reason and relied on intuition. I looked down at the base of the falls where the foam spread out like fog.

I told him, "A combatant is what you'll be."

He showed no emotion. "So it's the three of us."

"That's right."

He said, "Don't worry about Webb. He's served."

"In the military?"

"No, in West Virginia." Billy stood up and turned to the trail. "Let's go talk to him."

We met by the road, where Webb was singing a Willy Nelson song, head cradled against a flat-sided rock. Billy said, "Webb, come over here."

We formed a circle, and Billy had us recite an oath, binding us to each other and our mission.

21

The next day I phoned Webb, and we discussed a planning session for the invasion of the nest. He talked to Billy, who agreed to have the meeting at his home in the afternoon.

Webb and I arrived at the same time. Billy was on the porch. He said, "We should go out back, to the shed, away from Claire. She can't know anything about this."

The shed was of the Pennsylvania Dutch style, sturdy, with two doors folding out from the middle of one of its sides. Billy unlocked it, and we went inside. There were plenty of tools suspended from hooks on pegboard. On two walls were long wooden shelves near the ceiling upon which rested tool boxes and jars of screws and nails.

In the absence of chairs, we stood.

I had brought a tablet of drawing paper and a black felt-tip marker.

The meeting came to order. I asked, "Are you men ready?" When I saw nods, I drew Schroeder Street and the gang headquarters.

"The first factor is time. We go in tomorrow, just after nightfall, about 7:30. A day before they expect me to drop off a fifty-thousand-dollar ransom." Money in exchange for a human life was the equation. Having Brian in the middle of it seemed surreal. "They're never going to see a dime because even if they get the money, I believe they will keep Brian longer to collect more money."

Webb spoke up. "I think you're right, Doc. They'll see Brian as a kind of cash cow. With him, they'll always have the upper hand."

I said, "I've studied this a great deal, and when kidnappers ask for smaller sums, there is a high probability of a second ransom." I paused to wipe my sweaty brow. It was an unusually hot day.

"Second factor: transportation. We'll all drive in my car. It's fast and maneuvers well." I went to the paper and drew a passable tree. "This is the location of a crabapple tree, in front of the house next door to the nest. It will provide cover. We'll park there. I think it's highly unlikely anyone in the house will see us. Any questions?"

There were none.

I said, "Third factor: execution."

Billy looked distracted, out of focus.

I was concerned. "Billy, are you with me?" He turned to face me and nodded. "Just that this makes me feel like I'm back in school. Doc, you have to understand, plans are only plans. We'll have to play it by ear, depending on a lot of things." He folded his arms behind his neck in a relaxed pose. "That's all I had to say."

Webb said, "Billy doesn't listen well, Doc. He never did good in his schoolwork. He gave it to me, but I wasn't good either. Like the blind leading the blind."

I wanted to steer back on task. "Let's hope that's not what happens here."

Webb said, "Don't worry, Doc. We'll keep you in line."

"I know you guys will." I felt a surprising degree of rapport with both of these men. It could be very beneficial during the assault.

I said, "Execution is about weapons and assault. Webb, did you want to talk about this?"

"Okay." He walked to a ledge near the ceiling and pulled down a metal safe. After tumbling the lock, the tiny door opened out. Webb held a rag with something inside. When it was at eye level, he removed the covering. What became visible was a jet black pistol. He put it in my hand.

"Doc, introduce yourself to my Glock 17. The local cops use it. It's highly reliable, almost never misfires. It's deadly if you're within twenty-five feet of the target. You need a rifle for anything more than that."

"It's surprisingly light, Webb."

"It's made out of metal and plastic. Those Austrians know how to make guns. I never had it jam on me. If you're in a fight lasting a while, don't worry. It's got seventeen rounds a clip. Just what we'll need tomorrow."

I said, "Is it loaded?"

"It is. But the safety's engaged. So you can practice your shooting form. The key is keeping your balance. Like this." He demonstrated the proper stance, feet apart. "The backfire's pretty strong, but you'll get used to it." He handed it to me.

I said, "Webb, this is your gun. You're going to use it. I have no training whatsoever in using a handgun. Even if I did, I won't use it."

He was taken aback. "Why not?"

"Because I know without doubt I could never kill anyone."

He was surprised. "Then you're going into a battle with no weapon?"

I said, "I have a baseball bat in my trunk."

"But we're not going to be up against the Red Sox."

"I know how to use a bat to inflict bodily damage and take a person out of the fight." It was a lie. All I'd seen was a catcher knocked out by a batter's backswing.

"Doc, baseball bats are to protect yourself in case a thief comes into your house. You'll inflict a lot of pain, disable a person if you get close up. How're you going to get that close to a guy with a gun?"

Billy said, "Hold up there, Webb. We're not goin' into a full fledged battle here. This is a street fight with weapons. Both sides will be wantin' to kill each other. But if we place him correct, he can do harm with his bat."

"I don't like this, Billy. How can we put him in the right spot?"

"I'm telling you, he'll be there."

Webb mulled it over. "If you're sure." With his capitulation, I put the Glock back in the safe.

Webb said, "Billy, are you going in with your M16?"

I had read about them. I said, "M16? Aren't they military issue?"

Billy said, "They sure are. My dad, he used one in 'Nam. He killed a few NVA with it." He took it out of a long black chest and held it up to me. It was sleek with a long barrel and a magazine below.

I said, "Your father couldn't have brought this back from the war, could he?"

"He used to say a fairy dropped it from the sky into his yard. He just discovered it is all."

Webb smiled at Billy. "His old man, he was a mean son of a gun. Get it, Doc?"

I smiled. It was a passable joke at best.

We bantered on until there was a wrapping sound on the wall.

Billy reflexively hid the weapon under a piece of canvas. I shaded my eyes from the sunlight. In walked a bald man with a gruff look.

Billy said, "Uncle Ed, what are you doing here?"

"I'm checking up on you." He looked at me as if I were an annoying insect. He said, "Who are you?"

Billy intervened. "Ed, shut up and listen. I'm doin' what I'm doin'." He pointed at me. "And it ain't none of your business who he is."

The man looked at Webb. "Are the three of you planning something?"

There was venom in Billy's eyes. "Get out, Ed. I don't need no babysitter." His face nearly brushed up against the man's.

Ed's eyes narrowed. "After all Claire's been through." His voice raised. "She is going to know about this, and she won't stop until she gets the truth out of you. To stop you from doing something stupid."

He left, and I could see he was making a beeline to the house, to Claire.

As if all of the same mind, we gathered up the weapons, carrying them close to our bodies, and placed them in the trunk of the Audi. We got in, and I drove to the hotel. The elevator took me to my eighth floor room. Billy and Webb walked up the stairs, carrying the weapons inside my golf bag. They would need last-minute maintenance to insure their proper performance in tomorrow's activities.

22

It was Sunday night. The assault was about to happen.

The weather forecast called for a balmy spring evening, with a late cooling breeze off the harbor.

I pulled up on Schroeder, promising myself to focus on one thing at a time. We were within a few feet of the crabapple tree. I said, "Are you ready?" They were. I opened my door, and we left the car.

I was in the lead, carrying a baseball bat partially concealed under my coat. Webb was behind me, his Glock 17 in a shoulder holster on his right side. Billy, a few feet behind him, walked in a semicrouched position, pointing the rifle left to right and back again. The pace was deliberate.

I reached the edge of the property. There was a light on inside the house and the murmur from a TV on low volume. At the curb was an SUV.

The block was strangely silent, with no discernible movement. Even so, I worried that people could be watching out of their windows.

Behind me, I heard muffled voices.

"Give me your damn pistol, Webb. So's I can go up front. I can't see nothin' back here. Give it up!"

Webb said, "I'm sticking with the plan. Get away from me."

I was frustrated and angry. "Shut up, you two."

Billy had lost all composure. "Doc, listen. I can't shoot any a those bangers from here, much less see 'em. It's too damn dark." He turned to Webb. "You stay back with the rifle. Understand?" Webb had no response.

Billy said, "Doc?"

I told him, "I see your point. Webb, take the M16."

There was another muted and angry exchange. Billy approached me. "I'm gonna check out the backyard." He left and returned quickly.

"Nobody's back there." My heart was beating like it was going to jump out of my chest. He said, "Let's do it."

Billy and I reached the front porch. The ceiling light was out. There was a bit of illumination coming from a lamp inside the house. I looked about but could barely make out the shape of the house. Billy whispered, "Stand over there." He pointed to the joint between the steps and wall of the house. Carefully, I moved to it. I crouched down and assumed a kneeling position.

Billy walked slowly up the steps to the porch. On the right side of the door was a narrow window. He looked in, turned to me, and nodded his head.

I felt dizzy, close to fainting. The fear had me in its crosshairs.

Billy banged loudly several times on the window then ran down the steps and into an area of shrubs that hugged the porch.

Time stood still. Was nobody home? I began to hope so.

Two angry men came out the front door. "You little punks better get away from here. Don't let me catch you."

The other one said, "We better check around."

The one in front walked toward the steps. He was wearing slippers that emitted a slight cushioning noise. I raised up and drew the bat back. The dark was my cover.

I swung as hard as I could for his kneecaps. The blow was true. There was a pure cracking sound.

He let out a catlike sound. Billy said, "*Get down!*" I went low, feet on the top step.

Two shots rang out from the shrubs. The man fell headfirst down the steps.

The other one came forward and aimed his handgun in Billy's direction. I tried to hit him with the bat, but he was too far away.

He shot twice into the shrubs, blindly. There was a return of fire, and the man yelled, "Fuck!" He was hit. He released another round. There was an "Unnnnh." Billy had been shot.

I could feel the gunman's body faintly close. He held his bleeding shoulder, with his back to me. I ran toward him. He could hear my shoes against the wooden porch.

In a split second, he whirled to face me, the gun in his right hand.

I slammed the bat into his face. He fell back onto the porch like a bag of bricks. The gun dropped out of his hand, and his arms lay helpless at his sides. His eyes moved wildly back and forth, searching for his weapon.

I pulled the bat behind me and swung from my right side. The thick part near the end struck him cleanly on the jaw. He was out like a light. I bent over him. His eyes were closed. He was inert.

The violence was still palpable, as if it were a pack of wolves eating the flesh of dying animals. A tight knot formed in my stomach. I vomited acidic waste that burned my esophagus. My muscles were quaking.

I crabbed down the steps toward Billy. Webb was with him.

Billy's body was on its back. There was a red circle on the right side of his chest.

Feeling for a pulse, Webb said, "He's still alive. I have to get him to Hopkins ER."

The phone was deep in my pocket. I grabbed for it, took it out, and called 911.

Webb was whispering and screaming at the same time. "Billy! Billy! Stay with me!"

I looked back at the door, then the sidewalk. No attackers.

The Glock, black as night, was next to me, on the grass, pointing to the house as if telling me what I had to do. I picked it up. Webb was straddling his friend, crying.

I said, "He's been shot in the lung, Webb. They can save him. Don't worry."

He turned to me, then back at Billy.

I opened the screen door and went in, slowly, sweat rolling into my eyes.

Capo was on the phone, standing in the kitchen. His voice betrayed panic.

He punched in some numbers. "Answer the fucking phone!" He threw it against the wall. It cracked apart.

I sprung up on the counter, gun drawn. He saw it and grabbed my hand. We both fell on the floor, the gun rolling away toward the sink.

He was tall and lithe. The only chance I had was to free myself and grab the gun. He jumped atop me and banged my head into the floor. I felt stunned but had the strength to strike a roundhouse right to his head. He fell to my side, and I landed a glancing blow to his neck. There was a rapid counter punch to my cheek. I was swimming in a sea of sharks but managed to put my hands around his throat. He made a choking sound. I kneed him in the groin and pushed him off me.

Staying low, I moved toward the gun. There was a grasping and pulling at my ankles. It stopped my progress. I pounded my shoes against the floor and he lost his hold.

The gun was straight ahead. I grabbed it. It was cold and sleek. I lifted my self up and turned toward him. Holding the Glock with both hands, I aimed it at his heart. He was defiant.

"Fuck you, white man. You shoot me, and you'll never find your son. Never!"

I stood and approached him, pointing the gun barrel at his face. "Where is my son? Tell me now or I'll kill you. *Now!*"

His rage bubbled up like red lava, summoning a vile demon from within. It contorted his face. He rolled his body so that he could look right at me.

He said, "Put the goddamn gun down. You're not going to kill me. You can't. You don't have the balls to."

I shot him in the thigh, through muscle, avoiding the femur so he wouldn't pass out.

His voice seemed to come from a tunnel.

He mumbled, "You're crazy. And your goddamn son is dead."

I came around to his side, kicked him below the chest with full force. By now I was beyond every rule, every law I had ever obeyed. I blurted out, "I'll shoot every bone in your body, one at a time." The gun barrel was trained on his hip.

Naked fear opened his eyes, irises dilated like marbles. He blurted out, "He's in Philly. Twelfth and Race. An apartment above a store. That's all I know."

I checked his pockets. In his pants were a keychain, with a few car keys. I took them and left him writhing on the floor.

There was a door at the end of the hall that opened when I turned the knob. Running down the steps, I called out, "Brian. Where are you?" I spotted a place on the floor with four spikes, two rolls of masking tape, and four lengths of thick rope.

I ran frantically throughout the house, pounding walls and shouting my son's name.

Nothing.

Back in the kitchen, I could see that Capo wasn't going anywhere. He begged me to help him. I walked toward the front door.

It was time to leave. Reinforcements could be coming at any time.

I ran outside the front door toward Billy and Webb. Billy was making shallow, guttural sounds. Webb looked stricken. He was imploring his friend to keep breathing.

There was the howl of sirens fast approaching. I tapped Webb on the shoulder. He said, "Doc?" I told him I was going to Philadelphia, that Brian was there.

Sprinting toward the Audi, I removed its remote from my pocket. My hand was tight and shaking. I missed the handle in the dark. Finally it opened out. There was a bulge on the side of my body at the belt. The Glock. I removed the magazine and ran to the woods behind houses. Throwing the handgun with all my strength, I heard it hit the ground. In another direction I tossed the magazine.

I sprinted back to the car, revved the engine, and made a U-turn after the ambulance barreled by.

Driving too fast for city streets, I reached I-95 trying to control the adrenaline rush. My mind kept going back to the reality that this was the night. Any other night would be too late. Capo would call the kidnappers, and they would kill my son.

23

There was little traffic at this time of night. Trucks occupied the right lane of three. Economy cars, sedans, SUVs, and an occasional pickup played hopscotch. In Maryland, the fines were hefty for speeding and reckless driving. Impoundment was typical if speed exceeded more than twenty miles per hour over the speed limit.

I knew I had to be careful, but I started jockeying lanes to move ahead as much as reasonable. When there were no cars nearby, I brought the Audi up to eighty, in a speed-limit zone of sixty-five.

The last exit in Maryland was a mile ahead. After that, a toll plaza at the Delaware state line.

Reaching the toll plaza, I saw that there were only two pay-toll lanes open. About five cars waited in each one.

To save time, I decided to move to the left, where the EZ Pass route circumvented the toll plaza. I hadn't slowed down enough. The car skidded but managed to stay under control. "Way to go, Babe."

Through Delaware, I pushed the car up to 110. Overhead highway lights were spread further apart than in Maryland, so I cut on the high beams where necessary.

A Welcome to Pennsylvania sign came and went. Fatigue set in. My mind was aching for rest. I tried to counter the feeling, with minimal success, by stretching arms and legs.

I had an image of Brian calling out for help. Aloud, I said, "I'm coming, son. I'm coming as fast as I can. Whatever is happening to you will soon be over."

When I checked the rear view mirror, I saw the flashing red and blues of a highway patrol car.

My foot pushed further down on the pedal. When the speedometer dial reached 140, things were flying past at an alarming rate. I eased back to 130. With the help of the high beams, I anticipated a curve to the left where I-495 merged with I-95. The brakes screeched loudly, but the tires proved worthy, righting a skid.

Behind me the cop lights were smaller than before. He was losing ground. I could slow a little.

Suddenly another trooper's car shot out of the entrance ramp, close, about one-quarter of a mile behind me. He jerked it into the center lane, driving like an angry bull.

Instincts took over. I floored it, and the car lurched forward like a racehorse rounding the final turn. The trooper fell back, but not by far.

An exit appeared. I shifted lanes and got off, braking hard as the Audi screeched toward a stop at the first intersection. The light was blinking red. I turned a sharp left onto the cross street.

Traveling beyond the underpass, the road straightened up a steep hill. On the next corner was a supermarket. I turned left into a suburban community, where people parked on the streets and driveways by their houses.

At a four-way stop sign I turned left onto a narrow road, accelerating too fast.

The Audi sideswiped a white van.

The street became a circular cul-de-sac. I parked between a truck and a sedan, cut off the ignition and lights and waited.

Billy came into my thoughts. I saw him bleeding on the lawn. With every fiber of my being, I prayed he would survive. He had to. For his family. Because Claire loved him. Because he loved and protected his son. With his father's guidance, Drake would grow up to be a healthy human being.

I had set this all in motion. I had mitigated responsibility by telling myself that Billy and Webb had volunteered and that they knew the possibilities.

Billy joined for the purpose of resuscitating a life that war had shattered.

But regardless of his reasons, if he did not survive, I knew I would have his blood on my hands the rest of my life.

I was roused out of my reverie by the scream of a faint and distant police siren. It was moving away from the interstate.

It was time to leave. I doubled back and returned to the highway. Fearing another police car would find me, I had a strong impulse to abandon the highway and hide away along a deserted road. But I had to get to Philadelphia. Every second counted.

The GPS was set at the Race and Twelfth streets intersection on the north side of Center City. Despite my speed, I found the right exit.

It was only a few blocks to Race and four more to Twelfth. The neighborhood became seedier as I progressed.

I parked and walked to the intersection. There was a dollar store on one corner. It took up both floors. There were no apartments above it.

The next corner housed a run-down boxy building with gutters dangling from the roof. Pieces of a dull gray paint peeled off the decaying wood, testament to neglect.

The third corner held a dry cleaning shop. A window above had some plant boxes outside. There was a faint light in the apartment.

The last was an Army Navy store. Above it was an apartment, dark as a tomb.

I went back to the car and played with the GPS to see if it could tell me anything useful. It gave me an expanded map showing I was very close to Chinatown. Maybe some shops or restaurants were open. But at 1:00 in the morning, that was unlikely.

I needed two things. Somebody to get me into the apartment. And somebody to help me get Brian out.

24

Beyond a flight of five steps, on the pavement, I heard a plaintive voice. When I approached, I saw a disheveled woman in a shawl. Speaking calmly, I managed, "Are you all right?" She had high cheekbones, graying hair, and aging, leathery skin.

Her eyes flared. "Get away. I don't want your help."

I said, "I can call someone." Her expression turned to confusion. I took the phone out of my pocket and showed it to her. "Who can help you?"

She seemed to consider options, then turned her face away and fell silent.

Feeling stymied, I walked by her hastily. Up ahead, in the next block, were two men gesturing in exaggerated fashion with angry looks. I approached slowly, in a self-contained manner. One of them gave me a sideways motion with his arm. The other turned, then hastily made his way down the block.

I said, "Sir, I need some help."

He said, "It is not acceptable for you to approach me while I am talking with someone else." He was young, perhaps 25, Asian, with flowing black hair.

I said, "I am sorry. No harm was intended."

"What do you want?"

"My name is Daniel. Do you own this restaurant?"

"We are closed. Come back tomorrow."

I pleaded. "There is a woman down this street who is crying. She seems unable to stand. I think she is locked out of her home."

"I know her. All I must do is call her daughter, and she will have a place to stay tonight."

"Good. And there is something else. May I?"

"Get on with it. I am in a hurry."

"I need the name of a locksmith."

"What for? I don't know anything about you. Maybe you are a criminal."

"Let me explain. I live close to the waterfront. My house was broken into. They picked the lock completely off the door. Anybody can go through it now." The fantasy was becoming more real as I spoke. "The neighborhood has gone downhill since they changed the zoning. I have to protect what is mine."

"Why didn't you call the police? They could have sealed off the door."

"They could have. But I called them two days ago. I am still waiting."

He looked doubtful. "How do you expect me to believe you? This could be a lot of fiction."

"I wish it was fiction. Then it would all go away."

The man hesitated, staring off into the night. Suddenly he looked me in the eye. I returned the stare with a soft, sincere expression.

He removed a pad and pen from his shirt pocket, wrote down a name, address, and phone number and gave me the slip.

The address was in a community to the north, a little over four miles. I ran to my car and programmed the GPS.

It was a pinball ride, with a rash of one-way streets. But I reached the community without losing my way.

Big trees, spruces and maples, gave a feeling of grounding to an otherwise unremarkable working-class neighborhood. Some streets were cobblestoned, others paved. Street signs were nonexistent, as if they had become collector's items for teenagers.

The device told me I had reached destination. Running to the door, I fell over a kiddy car. Pain radiated from a shin. I got back on my feet, cursing my clumsiness.

There was no sound when I pressed the chime button. "Is anybody home? Hello?"

In the darkness, I fumbled about and located a knocker. I banged it with no restraint until a woman inside shouted, "Who is it? What do you want?"

"My name is Dr. Dan Davis. Is Marcus Heights home? I need a locksmith. It's late, I know, but this is an emergency."

"Go away. It's past midnight."

"Please. If I could just talk to your husband. Briefly."

A man's voice said, "Emily, go back to bed. I'll handle this." A light appeared on the porch, and I waited for something to happen. The familiar clicks of two deadbolts sounded out, and the door creaked open. A bearded young man said, "What is your problem? You come banging on my door like you're crazy."

"Please. I'm locked out of my house. In my place near Chinatown."

"Sleep in your car. Come back in the AM."

"I can't do that. The job needs to be done tonight. I'll pay you very generously. How does $500 cash sound?"

This aroused his suspicion. He put his hands on his hips and raised his voice. "I'll give you ten seconds to tell me why you're willing to pay me that much for a simple lock replacement."

I told him about Brian's situation. He pointed a finger at me. "Understand something. I have a wife and a little kid to support. I won't put myself in harm's way."

"Believe me, I completely understand you."

He said, "I'm going back in to get dressed."

Marcus came out putting his arm through a plaid shirt. He wore blue jeans, an unbuckled belt, and athletic shoes. At the step-up to his Dodge pickup, he tied his belt and shoelaces with the help of a street light. "Get in." He was all business.

We sat down in his vehicle and drove steadily to Twelfth and Race. He ignored the stop signs.

I said, "The place I need to find, it must be above that dry cleaner, or the Army Navy store. There are no other shops with apartments on top."

He pulled up to the cleaner's side lot and exited the truck. I met him at the front bumper. There were no cars in the lot. He said, "Come with me."

We headed around to a small back lot. In the dark, we nearly walked into a VW economy car. He said, "Do you think the people who have your son would drive this thing?"

"No. How would they take Brian here in a little car like this?" It displayed bumper stickers about conservation and animal rights. That was another excluding factor. "They wouldn't draw attention to themselves by placing these stickers on the car. I'm almost sure."

Marcus beelined toward a connecting driveway. He pointed. "Let's go that way."

We ran toward the back of the boarded-up building. The entire wall was painted a battleship gray. I could make out a window upstairs, painted black.

There was a vehicle in the driveway. It was covered over by a tarp. Only the tires were visible. We took the cover by its sides and pulled it vigorously upward. It came off after several yanks.

It was a dark blue van, about seven years old, with Maryland plates. Marcus took a high intensity flashlight out of his tool belt and shined it into the front and back seats. A bedspread with black patches shrouded the back floor. "That's not blood. It's paint or tar."

We walked to the building's rear door. Marcus tried to reason with me. "So you're really going in this building without a gun or common sense?"

"He's my son, Marcus. I've thought about it. This is the only way I can do it."

"Don't be a fool. We're going back to my place to get my .38."

"I have never fired a gun. What if I miss and shoot my son?" We were losing valuable time. To counter anxiety, I took a deep breath, but the injured ribs delivered a piercing pain. I hadn't taken enough pills. Straightening up brought the pain to a tolerable level.

I was scared and tired and hurting.

"Look, Dan, I'm going to call the cops." He was adamant.

"Marcus, listen to me. The last two times local police were involved in this kind of thing were fiascoes. Three years ago in Cheltenham, a kidnapped woman was shot to death by a psychopath because the police were overzealous. Last year, in Lansdale, a child was abducted. The FBI instructed the father to put out the bag for the kidnappers. The captors were on a hill, and they spotted four agents. They shot two, one fatally. The gunmen got away. The child is still missing."

Marcus sighed and held up his hands. "Okay, okay. It's your kid, your life. Just know this: I'm not going in, no way, no how."

He explained the general layout of upstairs apartments in this neighborhood. We agreed on a plan.

Marcus went to his truck. He came back with a metal box. Sorting through the contents, he picked out a few and schooled me in the use of tools I would need to remove the apartment lock.

We walked together to the door, and he showed me where to shine the flashlight. Then he looked in the narrow gap between the door and its frame. "If this is a new lock, we have a problem." With a crow bar, he jimmied the door so that there was a slightly wider gap between the door frame and the door. After putting aside the crowbar, he picked up a metal-cutting saw and placed it in the gap.

He said, "I hope to God this doesn't wake them up."

The saw tore through the chain above the lock but failed to cut through the bolt.

Marcus sat on the grass. "Don't say anything."

He closed his eyes and silently spoke to himself. Minutes went by. I was jumping out of my skin.

His eyes opened. "It all comes down to the wood in the frame. If it's intact, we can't get in. If it's decomposing, we can." He turned to the tool box and fished out a crowbarlike tool. With the claw pointing toward the frame, he carefully inserted it. He grunted as he applied maximum force. Nothing happened. A second effort produced a tearing noise as the frame gave in at the lock and a snapping sound as the bolt freed itself, falling to the floor with a clang.

Marcus tossed the bar backwards. All that was left was to push the door out of our way. It opened without a fight.

I breached the entrance.

Marcus leaned his head into the darkness. "Listen, I'm telling you. Stay focused. Adjust the plan as needed."

The hallway was about ten feet wide. On the floor were black and white tiles.

The fourteen steps were covered in a faded red rug. I proceeded to the top, where a dim light shone from a floor lamp by the wall.

I took out the flashlight and found the apartment door. Fumbling in the wrong pocket, I dug into the correct one and removed two small screwdrivers and a putty knife. I applied them as Marcus instructed and defeated the cheap lock in seconds.

The door moved outward with a slight creaking sound.

I was through. Leaving the door slightly open, I took a few cautious steps forward.

The bathroom was to the left. It was nearly pitch black except for a night light plugged in above the baseboard.

When I stopped moving, there was the sound of a fan. I wanted to make sure no one was awake. Kneeling in front of a closet, I kept still. After five minutes, nothing had moved.

Beyond the bathroom, to the right, was a living room with a couch, end table, lamp, and TV.

I continued down the hallway. There was a door on the left, shut tight. I took the knob and opened it. There was no light in the room. I groped about for a light switch and found one.

My son was on the floor, semiconscious. His wrists were tied tightly with ropes. Their other ends were tied to the legs of an upright steam radiator. Around his ankles were heavier ropes tied to spikes hammered into the floor. Gray duct tape sealed over my son's mouth. His breathing was faint.

There were purple bruises on his face and neck. I took his pulse. It was fast, 124 beats per minute. I rubbed his cheeks. They were very dry, almost scaly. He was   dehydrated.

His eyes opened. They were swollen and red with broken blood vessels.

"Son, you're going to be okay. I'm getting you out of here."

Brian's eyes showed fear, then surprise. I said, "I'm taking off the tape and ropes." I placed an index finger to my lips. "Make no noise." He nodded. I ripped off the tape. He winced in pain. His lips were white and cracking. I looked around but found no water.

Carefully, I untied the ropes.

We crawled in tandem along the floor. There were footsteps. The room door was open about a foot. A man was coming out of the corner room behind us. I could see his slippers stop moving under the door.

"Hey, Harvey, how come we got no food in this goddamn place? You said you went to the grocery store."

No response. The man in the hall went into a room to the left. There was the sound of running water. A cough, then the pop of a bottle cap. His footsteps proceeded our way.

I moved behind the door, pulling Brian by his shirt. His face contorted in pain.

The man outside grasped the doorknob and poked his head in the room. "What the—"

His bottle spilled beer and foam. He saw Brian in the shadows.

The man was short and stocky. I rose up and grabbed him by the collar.

We wrestled for the upper hand. Out of nowhere he jammed a pistol against my face. I went stock still.

"You like savin' people? Well, let's see if you can save yourself from a shallow grave."

I went for a screwdriver. When it was in my hand, I wound back my arm, and lunged forward and stuck it into his belly. And stuck it again. His eyes bulged, and he dropped the weapon. He groped for me in vain. I launched an uppercut, landing it to his chin. It tore off skin from my knuckles. With my other hand, I landed a left to the wound. He grimaced in pain, but kept his footing. I grabbed him by the calves and pulled up as hard as I could. His body elevated, then he fell headfirst to the wood floor. He stayed down, grimacing in pain. Blood flowed from his scalp. He stayed down, grimacing in pain.

The gun lay on the floor near my son. I put it between belt and pants.

Brian was struggling to get up. I said, "Stay down, Brian. Stay down."

I looked out the door. No movement.

Kneeling down by my son, I saw him wince, perhaps in pain, or fear of violence and recapture. I could only guess at what he had endured.

"Brian, we're doing the alligator walk." In Florida, as a child, he had enjoyed riding on my back.

"Grab my shoulders. Hold on." In a few seconds we were a team. "That's it, son. You're doing great."

I crawled us through the open door and into the hall.

The stairs looked to be about twenty-five feet ahead. They were our path to escape.

Fear slowed my progress, making my limbs feel rigid and useless. I was breathing fast. Necessity led me to stop for a short break.

I resumed moving. We arrived at the steps.

"Hey, you!" A shot discharged behind us, then another. They missed. I released Brian's leg grip and jumped on top of him to take the next shot. Brian somehow sprung himself free of me and rolled into the lamp stem. It fell downstairs, *boom-boom-boom*. We followed, descending into opaqueness, halfway to the bottom. More shots rang out.

Something hot and penetrating whistled through my upper arm. I looked behind me. He was barefoot, wearing pajamas, checking his gun. It clicked.

I reached for my weapon, but it stayed lodged under my belt. Changing position, I tried again but pulled too hard, and it became a projectile flying toward the ceiling, then falling on the stairs. I lunged for it but could not see where it was.

The shooter ran toward the gun. He was close.

"Dad! Hold on!" Brian kicked the wall, and we went slaloming down the steps, until we reached the floor.

There was a shot fired from behind, followed by two shots from below. I looked to my side at the gunman. He grasped his chest and fell sideways, trying in vain to grab the railing. He came down on top of me, his body lifeless. I rolled over, and he fell off me onto the tiles.

I turned my head. There was a visage below sinking to his knees.

"Marcus!"

He dropped the gun and braced his fall with extended hands. He looked toward me. "I told you I wasn't going to get involved."

My throat was raspy but I managed, "Are you okay?"

"Yeah. Mighty scared though."

25

Two techs in pale blue shirts and white pants placed my son on a mobile bed. A doctor performed the initial examination in the emergency room.

Another doctor ushered me off to a small room where I provided her with facts I could recall about Brian's medical history, disappearance, and captivity.

Slowly, my son responded to the therapies and regained his former health.

I waited for him to tell me what happened. One day, when we were home, he was ready.

He did go to Baltimore to be with Sherrie, hoping they could renew their relationship. At that time, he did not know about her descent into drug dependency.

From the start, he saw that she had changed. That first day, without any warning, she spun out of control, telling him to get out of her house.

He left, then returned with food, and she let him in. But her flare-ups continued. She was having severe mood swings and did not sleep much. At random times, Sherrie disappeared and was gone for most of the day or night. When she came home, it was clear to Brian that he was not to ask her where she had been.

There were strange people coming to her place and staying for hours. If they were talking together, they stopped when Brian entered the room. He saw them taking drugs, mainly pills, from their pockets.

Concluding that Sherrie was incapable of behaving normally until becoming drug free, Brian decided to leave unannounced. As he was packing, she came into the room. She was convincingly apologetic.

The next morning, Sherrie said she wanted him to give her a ride to Southwest. She denied it was to purchase drugs. Brian knew she was lying but went along with her anyway because he realized that trying to change her mind would be futile. Even if he turned his back on her, she would use someone else to do her dirty work.

They drove down Baltimore Street and turned at an intersection occupied by a tall African Methodist church. A few blocks down, Sherrie told him where to park. She became impatient with his driving and opened the door while the car was still in motion.

Dogs inside fences barked as she ran up steps to a man on the porch. After a brief exchange, he led her through the front door.

On the way home, Sherrie wanted to take a shortcut just in case police cars had set up a blockade on Lombard.

A few blocks into a wrong turn, it became apparent to Brian that they were lost. Sherrie told him to shut up, just drive.

They went down streets where there were no traffic lights or stop signs. Brian felt increasingly worried.

As he drove slowly by a boarded up warehouse, a gunshot rang out ahead. Seized by impulse, Brian jumped out of the car and moved forward. Sherrie ducked down under the dashboard.

In the darkness, Brian crouched behind a fire hydrant. When he peered out, he saw a man lying dead on the sidewalk about a hundred feet away. Standing above the dead body was a man pulling off the victim's vest bag. He threw the murder weapon, a handgun, down a gutter and hoisted the bag over his shoulder.

Brian followed the shooter up a street to a block of row houses.

A police siren grew louder, then abated as a squad car pulled up beside the body. The cop inspected it with a flashlight.

Hearing the footsteps of the running man, the officer ordered the thief to stop. The man kept running, and the cop fired and missed. He retreated to his car to call for backup.

Brian ran behind the cover of bushes and trees in pursuit of the running man. As he hustled up a hill, Brian heard two more patrol cars approach. There was little time to catch up to the man. With no plan, Brian was caught up in the excitement of the moment.

The thief must have feared he would be shot or apprehended. He threw the bag over a wrought iron fence, then ran around the corner, cursing his misfortune. Brian accelerated. Again, there was a flurry of errant shots from the police cars.

In one mad motion, Brian hurdled over the fence. He grabbed the bag and slung it over his shoulder. Finding a gap in the fence, he squeezed through it and continued up the street until he took a few seconds to catch his breath.

There was conversation above. Looking upward, Brian saw two old men standing on a second floor porch, staring at him. One of them was talking on a cell phone.

The bag was heavy, but less so when he shifted it to his hand and forearm. He ran like a halfback to the mouth of an alley.

Counting streets, he successfully navigated a path around the police back to his car. When he opened the driver door, Sherrie was still under the front seat, crying helplessly. He told her she was going to be okay, then threw the bag on the backseat.

Key in the ignition, he waited for the police to move forward in search of the running man. When they did, he took a U-turn and drove away, powered by the thrill of escape.

He was approaching a commercial street, but as he turned and checked the rear view mirror, it reflected high beams moving fast toward him.

Brian took evasive action, driving down several narrow streets. But he couldn't shake the pursuing vehicle. In a desperate state, Brian drove down a dead end too fast and crashed the Toyota head-on into a wooden wall. The car bounced backward.

Stunned and in a semiconscious state, he felt a man's large hands dragging him out of the car. The passenger seat was vacant.

Lying on grass, he felt a surge of heat. Huge yellow flames engulfed his car.

Through the flames, he saw Sherrie on the grass and a big black man standing over her, yelling that he would kill her if she told the police about him or his accomplice.

He recalled little after this, only bits and pieces. People yelling, cursing him, threats to cut off body parts. A money bag in the back seat of his car. Feeling thirsty, often. Being thrown into a car trunk and driven somewhere. Waking up while being tied to stakes.

EPILOGUE

I resumed my Rockville practice. Some clients who were unwilling to wait through my absence had found other therapists. I had to scramble about for new patients.

When the time seemed right, I drove up to Baltimore. Billy had survived the bullet that punctured a lung. He spent four days in intensive care with his life in the balance. Claire was justifiably furious with me. I apologized to her but never expected that she would forgive me for placing her husband in the line of fire. A year later, she wrote me a letter explaining that she had given up being angry with me.

Billy found employment as a construction worker. The job gave him back some of the sense of self he had lost in the war.

Sherrie had given in to drug addiction and died of a heroin overdose.

No charges were filed against Webb, Billy, or me, even though we assaulted three men at the nest and one died.

In the drug business, death is a private affair. The dead are buried, and their death is kept quiet.

But the home invasion at a gang's house was reported in an article in the first section of the *Baltimore Sun*. The incident created quite a stir but faded quickly from the city's consciousness.

Webb is well. After Billy's shooting, he swore off of violence and became a volunteer at a nursing home. He also drops in on sick children to cheer them up.

Novelli gave me a heated lecture for taking the law into my own hands. When he calmed down, he said to me, "Don't tell anyone this. I understand what you had to do. It was about family."

He led an investigation that never left the back shelf of a police evidence room.

It was all a nightmare that I would never forget. But I knew, if I had to do it again, I would.

Without hesitation.

ABOUT THE AUTHOR

William Shore, a transplanted Easterner, is a psychologist in private practice in New Mexico. Recently, he picked up the pen to pursue a lifelong dream of writing fiction.

Bill is particularly interested in portraying the plagues of substance abuse and gang violence in urban America.

Aside from writing novels, Bill has composed short stories on a wide range of topics.

CPSIA information can be obtained
at www.ICGtesting.com
Printed in the USA
LVHW030238100623
749126LV00001B/175

9 781634 175388